THE UNIVERSAL PHYSICS OF ESCAPE

THE UNIVERSAL PHYSICS OF ESCAPE

Winner of the 2015 Press 53 Award for Short Fiction

To Dylan,

Best wishes,

Betsy Gonzalez

10. Oct 2015

ELIZABETH GONZALEZ

Press 53
Winston-Salem

Press 53, LLC
PO Box 30314
Winston-Salem, NC 27130

First Edition

The Universal Physics of Escape
Winner of the 2015 Press 53 Award for Short Fiction

Cover design by Sarah Gonzalez

Author and cover artist photos by
Tiffany Shelly Photography

In the story "The Universal Physics of Escape," references from the
following sources used by permission:

"The Octopus: A Model for a Comparative Analysis of the Evolution of Learning
and Memory Mechanisms," copyright © 2006 Marine Biological Laboratory.

"Octopus Arms Found to Have 'Minds' of Their Own," by John Roach,
copyright © 2001 National Geographic Society.

Cephalopod Behaviour, by Roger T. Hanlon & John B. Messenger,
copyright © 1996 Cambridge University Press.

"Hapalochlaena Lunulata," Kelly Ray,
copyright © 2014 Regents of the University of Michigan.

Printed on acid-free paper
ISBN 978-1-941209-31-8

for Doddoggie and the Queen

Acknowledgments

The author thanks the editors of the publications listed below for first publishing the following stories:

"0 = 1," *Solstice* Summer 2013

"Departure," *Pear Noir!* Issue 5, Spring 2011

"Half Beat," *Greensboro Review* Issue 85, Spring 2009

"Here," *Wag's Revue* Issue 5, March 2010

"The Reclamation Specialist," *Post Road* Issue 18, Winter 2009

"Shakedown," *Tusculum Review* Issue 8, April 2012

"The Speed of Sound," *Hunger Mountain* Issue 16, December 2011

"Trajectories," *Trigger* Issue 2, January 2012

"Weather," *Sycamore Review* Vol. 20.2, Fall 2008

CONTENTS

Shakedown   1

Weather   19

$0 = 1$ 33

Half Beat   39

Here   57

The Reclamation Specialist   61

Anatomy of Stone   77

Departure   87

The Speed of Sound   91

Trajectories   107

The Universal Physics of Escape   115

A note from the author   153

Author biography   155

Cover artist biography   157

SHAKEDOWN

The men call her she, just like a ship, and they work on her through the night while rain marks time on the metal roof of the shed. Finney pulls the whistle cord and she emits a clank, a rattle like coins falling into a can or an anchor being hoisted. Again he pulls, and gets this awful clatter, but underneath they all hear it—a cough, a breath, patchy at first, then growing louder, unmistakable. It fills the shed and spills out the door, pours out over the lights of Altoona, echoes off the invisible hills. Their hearts surge, tears come, but they are old friends, comrades in this collusion; they're all pulling out their hankies and hawking snot and wiping crazy tracks on their faces and nobody says a word.

They love her in the old, high way of love, a thing you can't rightly do anymore, sappy as a sailor's salute. But these men are pot-bellied and past caring. They love this train, love her practically, as it should be, with wrenches and torches and grease, the kind of love they gave their wives and children, for all that's worth, forty years of lunches in tin boxes and coffee from a Thermos, a greasy hat on a peg by the door, blackened overalls propped in the corner.

How many said it could not be done? An engine like this is meant to run; sitting idle is hard on her. But this is hard coal country, where somebody misread a map once and they blasted too far west and poked a hole in the Susquehanna—a mile-wide river and it was like somebody pulled the plug on a bathtub. And nobody called the federal government; no one hauled in the National Guard. They threw in four hundred boxcars to try to plug the hole, boxcars that upended and circled the vortex before disappearing into the churning water like so many children's toys. It flooded till the mines filled and there was nothing left to flood, and then everybody came in and picked up the pieces. Compared to that, what's a seized-up engine? It's just a matter of work, that's all anything ever is, all it ever was.

He's out in the front yard in his underwear, pistol in his right hand, bathrobe flapping in the wind behind him like a cape. The man from up the hill called again, and said he's coming down to shoot the dogs, and Pap says this morning he's going to shoot that cowardly bastard once and for all.

He turns and glares, *stay back.* Amy pulls her brother aside, but within moments they're all peering out the window again, peeping out from the sheers. He scans the broad slope of lawn, the woods encircling it, his mouth drawn down, eyes in a squint. When the wind picks up his hair it's transparent, like feathers. He reads a lot of westerns, goes through them like Rolaids. They're printed on paper so cheap they're weightless, and turn stiff and brown within a matter of weeks. When you pry one open, it buckles and cracks.

This time, his dreams become real: he has invoked the law. Gravel pops down below, then a cop car appears, slowly creeping up the hill. Duke and Duchess bark. He stands there, holding the pistol out from his thigh, doesn't even think, evidently, of closing his robe. The holster would have been a nice touch, but he'd come out in too much of a hurry. He maintains his position, scowling at the woods while the trooper climbs the hill and stops before him.

"Mr. Bent," the cop tells him, "it is against the law to threaten to shoot someone. If you do," he continues, waving away what her grandfather starts to say, "you will be arrested. I understand you're upset about the calls, in which case I'd advise you to file a complaint with the phone company—"

"A phone complaint?" he sputters. "You go up there and give him the message—I ain't fooling around. If I see him on my property, *I* am *going* to *shoot* him," he says, pointing up at the cop with his stumpy index finger. "I'm eighty-five years old. I got nothing to lose."

"Mr. Bent, as I said, it is against the law to make terroristic threats—" the cop begins to say, but her grandfather cuts him off.

"Oh, that ain't no threat."

Eventually the cop gives up. Pap stands, unmoved, watches the car make its slow retreat down the rutted drive. He makes one last survey of the woods, glaring hard into the trees, before turning back toward the house.

"Chickenshit," he mutters as he mounts the little steps from the foyer, holding hard to the wrought iron rail. "Sure, he's big on the phone, cursing out an eighty-year-old woman—he calls again, Alma, you hand the phone right to me, the little, aw," he says, left hand propped against the wall, body swaying as he pries his feet out of his slippers. "I'd like to choke him, actually, shooting's too good." He straightens up, yanks on his robe. "If I could take off a kneecap, that'd be better yet, but at my age, it's torso shots only!" he says, shaking his pistol at the ceiling. He appears to have forgotten the guy up the hill, he's so delighted with his performance.

"Is that loaded, Daddy?" her mother asks.

"Can I hold it, Pap?"

"Huh?" he says. "No, Stevie, no. Of course it's loaded," he tells her mother. "You never point an unloaded gun at somebody. That'd be crazy."

He smells like hair oil and liniment, her grandfather. He does unthinkable things with phlegm.

He keeps the idle on his car set high because he feels it runs better that way, and when he turns the key it starts right up. As a result, it tends to lurch into gear and accelerate whenever his foot isn't firmly applied to the brake. He also has a habit of driving with his left tire on the center line of the road. When Amy brings it to his attention ("Pap—ooh! You're on the line!") he tells her, "Of course I am. I use the line to sight by. That's the only way I can see where I'm going." Between that and the sheer heft and bulk of his powder blue Thunderbird, he's a regular cannonball rolling through the streets of Cope. She wonders how it is that he has never hit anyone on these narrow streets, every one of them pitched and winding and hemmed in so close by porches you can read the headlines on people's papers while you wait at the lights.

Her mother sent her to the bank with him, which tells you the hierarchy of things—she doesn't like him driving alone. Of course, there's little Amy can do for him from the passenger seat except make these periodic exclamations, and wave to the people they offend. And be that thing he craves most, an audience.

He stomps on the accelerator, punches the little lighter button, gives the steering wheel a jerk, hears her head bump the window. He looks over, smiles, heh. "Watch your head."

"Pap!" she cries, and throws a hand up on the dash.

"I see him, I see him," he says, braking lightly and swerving around a man crossing the road. She sees the man whirl around, shrinking in the sideview mirror, and flip them the bird as they hurtle on. He brakes for Third Street, rummages in his shirt pocket, pulls out a smoke, squints up at the light. Music drifts down from an upstairs window. He snaps a lever and the turn signal chimes, ancient and mechanical, *cadink cadink, cadink cadink.*

"The first time I came out here, I came for a loan," he says. The lighter hisses and snaps. He takes a few rapid lip puffs, exhales. "I got all dressed up, put on a suit coat and a nice white shirt and combed my hair real nice, and I go in there with my hat in hand and smile at everybody and they say, 'Oh, Mr. Bent. We're sorry, we can't give you a loan without any collateral.' So I say, 'If I had collateral, why would I need a loan? I already sold everything I got.' And you know what the guy says to me? 'That's very amusing, Mr. Bent. I'm sorry we can't help you.'"

He turns the wheel and the hood of the T-Bird noses up for a moment like a speedboat before plunging down Third Street, thumping over the railroad tracks.

"And you know what? He still manages the bank today. Only now he's *so* nice to me," he says with a wry little smile. "Now I go in there like this, dressed like a bum, with greasy shoes and holes in my shirt and my Purolator hat and they say, 'Oh, Mr. Bent. Right this way, Mr. Bent. How are you today?'" he mimics, playing a teller now and batting his eyes as he always does for the ladies' parts. "'Oh, I'm just fine, thank you,' I say, and hand over the envelope. 'I have a deposit. I'm sorry, I didn't have time to count it,'" he says in his meek old-man voice, and at this he smirks.

"Right," she says on cue. It's a family joke, and one she's heard many times. They rocking-horse over a curb, maneuver around the bank. A pellet of ash drops to the floor and rolls back and forth on the floor mat under his feet. He drives his foot onto the brake and releases, and the T-Bird putters, cowed, into a parking space.

"Know what the difference is?"

Here, no answer. Just a look.

"Money," he says with a flick of the wrist that says, "end of story."

"Go for the buck!" he tells her, spiraling his index up into a little exclamation point. He lost the end of that finger in a grinder some years back, and the mutation has proven useful, serving as a visual aid and providing the perfect foundation for a pool bridge. To her it seems custom-made for finishing his stories: up comes the finger, out comes the moral of the story. For there is always a moral to his stories.

This morning, her first moves under steam. She nosed out of the shed, quietly chuffing, made twelve feet of track and blew a boiler relief valve. Now she's swallowed up in steam, restless clouds of steam, and Warren has also found leaks in the tender. They'll have to drain the boiler and the tender, dump the fire.

Warren's a professional. He takes it calmly enough, although this is a setback, a major setback. They may make Sunday and they may not. He talks to Junior about the tender welds and checks in on Mike and Lloyd, who are working on the boiler, then goes into the shop to call his wife. In fourteen months he's been home to California only for holidays and an occasional weekend.

Every time he disassembles a train—and he's overseen several of these restorations—he experiences a dull panic, surveying an entire building littered with rusted parts, each bearing a little oak tag label on a string. It lingers as an uneasiness through the painting phase, and subsides only when they begin bolting on the lights and bells and brass plates. It's not the size of the task, that would be one thing— it's because there's something in the assembled train that wasn't on the floor with the parts. It's like holding up a jacket and a pair of arms sliding in and a live person walking away—he, the jacket holder, is astonished every time.

Every morning her grandfather leaves before seven to open the shop, a hydraulics business situated at the foot of the hill, like base camp. It's his third business, founded after the first two failed, which he launched after the Pennsylvania Railroad put him on furlough in '29, a series of calamities that propelled him to his eventual success. He loves to portray himself as the mean old tyrant, and to horrify Amy and Steve with stories of how he harasses the guys down there. "They stand behind the counter and stare," he tells them. "I come up behind this guy today and here he is, just standing there looking at the phone like he's waiting for it to ring. Know what I told him? 'Do me a favor.'

"'Yeah?' he says.

"'When you die, fall over so I know you're dead.'"

"Oh, Pap," Amy says.

"It's true—these young guys today, I tell you, they just don't have the drive. I'm walking behind one of them the other week—the new guy, what a slouch—he's back in the shelves, and he's walking so slow I almost tripped over him. I kid you not—I never saw a guy could walk that slow." He jumps out of his chair to demonstrate. "Twenty-some years old, and the guy's walking, like a sleepwalker," he says, plodding across the kitchen, "and I'm behind him, like this," and he throws out an arm and starts dodging and dancing like a football player looking for an opening, "and I'm eighty-five years old.

Finally I couldn't stand it anymore, I said, 'Outta me way, Jesus! I got stuff to do.'"
"No wonder they always look so happy," Amy says, putting away her homework.
"Yeah, and he turned and stared at me, like this." He stares, mouth hanging open, at an imaginary version of himself walking by. "An eighty-five-year-old man. I tell you, I could run circles around these guys. If I'd had the advantages they have?" He shakes his head, settles back in his chair. "These guys today don't have the drive, the desire or the determination," he says, counting on his fingers. "The three Ds. I tell you, Amy, you can do anything you want— anything—if you just have the three Ds. You got to—you got to work for it, that's all."

He reaches for his pill basket, starts turning the bottles, looking for his stomach medicine. "You got to fight, fight, fight for what you want," he says, almost to himself. "For every last thing you want."

When Amy and Steve were little, he used to pull his upper teeth loose and chase them around the pool table, moaning and gnawing at them until they would crawl underneath, rolling from side to side out of his reach. Finally he'd catch a leg, drag them out one by one, screaming, and tickle them until their ribs hurt.
"A good pool player doesn't make hard shots," he teaches them. "He sets up every shot to be an easy one. When you go to these tournaments, you don't see them making triple banks or jumping balls, not when they're playing for money. They don't even like a long shot, like that, that's too much green," he says, waving his hand dismissively at his shot at the far end of the table. "They just go around, bump bump bump, like it's nothing. They save their tricks for the exhibitions."

It's a regulation slate table, bought from a pool hall that went out of business, with big aluminum pockets, each bearing a bright orange number five. Pool is the closest thing to a hobby he has, and he only plays it because at various times in his life he's been able to rely on it for quick income. Even at eighty-five, with uncertain balance and glasses so thick they make his eyes look like silver dollars—glasses that rarely see a clean handkerchief—he can still clear the table. He bends and shoots. The cue ball stops, transfers its momentum neatly to the nine, which smacks the back wall of the pocket and promptly sinks.

At eighty-two her grandmother still goes to work with him six days a week, coming and going faithfully with her Thermos and lunch bag, her colorful pants suits adorned with holiday pins and flowing scarves. For lunch she carries doughnuts and sticky buns, leftovers wrapped in foil with all the shine crinkled out.

Unlike Pap, Amy's grandmother likes to keep a few things to herself. It hadn't even occurred to Amy that she must be dyeing her hair until they'd moved in with them last fall, and she'd noticed the monthly color fluctuations from auburn to brown, and the halo of white that emerged between treatments. She's a half-secret woman of a grandmother, a woman with a bit of the magician in her, harkening from a time of girdles and hairpins and brow pencils, when secret-keeping was as integral to womanhood as stockings. To Amy, Nanny is theater and magic, and her bureau is her stage, her magic trunk. It's a haphazard wonder, dusted with body powder and overflowing with lipsticks, gilt brushes and combs, outrageous costume jewelry, candies, coffee-stained letters and photos and post cards, and it smells of her, of compact powder and perfume tinged with urine, and a hint of the tobacco that spills from her cigarettes.

She's a match for the old man, Nanny. She smokes Pall Mall unfiltereds.

"Seventy-eight miles an hour? That ain't nothing for a K-4," her grandfather says, tossing the newspaper onto the table. "Me and Mason topped that lots of times. Shoot, a K-4 can do that up Shickshinny Hill." He watches Amy's father read for a moment, then turns to Amy and Steve.

"That time, when we blew out of Cope late," he says, opening a Tastykake krimpet. "The train was late out of Wilkes-Barre—all but an hour late, which was unheard of for the passenger trains in those days—Mason was furious. So anyway, there were these two businessmen standing on the platform dressed real fancy, you know, and they're making fun of Cope, making fun of the railroad, and then they turn around and see Mason and me in our coveralls. So one of them says to Mason, 'You think this Toonerville Trolley'll make Philadelphia on time?'

"And Mason says, under his breath, 'If she holds together we will.'" He rubs his fingers together over a saucer, trying to dislodge the clingy krimpet wrapper. He shakes his hand, looks over at Steve, exasperated, until he gets his laugh, finally gets the wrapper to drop to the plate.

"So, when that train hit the station we're up in the engine and I'm just banking coal, 'cause I know what I'm in for, and Mason's throwing down sand, and soon's he got the signal we blasted out of there; he practically knocked me back into the tender, and you know, Paul," he says as her father looks up from the paper, "that engine never slipped an inch. We shot out of there like a bat out of hell and never slowed down. Well, we get down around Poorman's Curve, and I can feel her leaving the tracks. So I'm getting a little nervous, because you know I'm standing like this," he says, getting up, wiping his hands on his pants and going to the center of the kitchen. "You're just perched up there on the gangway between the engine here and the tender over here, and you're shoveling coal into the firebox and the platform's open on either side; there's nothing to hold onto, and you're getting jostled this way and that—it was hair-raising, let me tell you. There were some guys couldn't stand to do it in the dark. So when I felt the engine leaving the tracks, I yelled to Mason, 'How far does she go before we tip?' And you know what he says?

"'Twenty-four inches—we're only going twenty-one!'"

"Jeez," her father says, shaking his head.

"You ain't kidding," Pap says, still straddling the carpet. Nanny sidesteps him, rolling her eyes, deposits a tippy melmac bowl full of macaroni and tuna salad on the table. "Oh, sit down and eat," she says, poking him with her elbow as she heads back to the stove. She has a gruff way with him, and since he wants gruffness, it's oddly affectionate. He's like a tough old weed she has to keep yanking out, or he'd grow all over everything.

"Two hundred-thirty tons of engine hopping almost two feet off the tracks, and I'm standing on the damn thing freestyle, shoveling coal," he says, taking his seat again, his eyes crinkled and happy and white-blue now, like worn denim.

"We got clocked south of Reading between two towers, eleven miles apart, at seven minutes. Ninety-five miles an hour. And that was on a curve—on the straights he had it over a hundred, easy. We got disciplined for it, lost a week's pay. But, would you believe it, we whistled into Philadelphia *on time*. He made up fifty-five minutes on a two-and-a-half-hour trip. So we get there and out come those two businessmen, and they are madder than hell. Here all the luggage came out of the racks and it was quite a commotion back there, and the one guy comes over to Mason and says,

'You're crazy. I'm never riding with you again!' And Mason just looks at him and says, 'You made it to Philadelphia on time.' Ha!"

He flicks an ash. He has an odd way of thumbing his ashes up toward the ashtray from several inches away, a feat he performs with admirable accuracy, the burn holes in the vinyl tablecloth attesting to the occasional miss.

"There was only a handful of guys in the world, even back then, who could do that with an engine," Pap says, getting serious again.

"Would you like to go see it, Dad?" her mother asks, looking at the article. "We could watch it come into Bellefonte."

"It's a drive," Pap says, shaking his head. "Two hours at least."

"It's Sunday. We have all day. We can go, can't we, Paul?"

"Sure."

"That would be something," Pap says, taking the paper from her, looking at the photo, "to see one run again."

Every night around nine he goes down to the shop to check on the place. Kids are always parking down there, smoking their loco weed and smashing beer bottles in the parking lot. That night, sure enough, there's a pickup truck behind the garage, pulled up against the building.

He brings the T-Bird up alongside, a couple of car widths away, gets out and walks over to the truck.

"Shove off," he says to the kid in the driver's seat. "This is private property."

"Hey, check this out," the kid says, gesturing with his Yuengling bottle. "What're you going to do, little old man, you going to kick my ass?" His friend laughs, a little cough, says, "You better go home, dude."

"Yeah," the driver says. "You better."

He laughs along. "That's right; I'm just a little old man. But this little old man," he says, drawing his pistol out of his pants, "got six little helpers." He levels the gun at the kid's head, cocks it. Eight feet. Can't miss.

It has the desired effect. The kid drops his beer, starts cursing like he's praying, the truck wheels snort and spin, gravel spatters the building and pings the old man in the shin, and all the while he stands there, tracking the little punk, his mouth drawn down in his happiest, grimmest gunslinger smile.

He follows the sound of their retreat, their engine slowing for the turn, rumbling under the bridge, then whining out onto 61 and north until it disappears. Dust rises, drifts in a cloud over the pair of ancient gas pumps down the lot. Gnats zigzag drunkenly under the lights. Foam from the beer hisses and soaks into the gravel, a spreading stain.

He tilts his head, eyes crinkling up—he can't help it—and shrugs. "You just have to reason with people," he says to the evening, audience of the moment. He watches the wheeling insects, the old pumps for a minute before he releases the hammer, tucks the pistol into his pants and walks slowly back to the T-Bird.

The men have been working for more than forty hours on naps and scalded coffee, soggy cheese steaks and stale, picked-over doughnuts, but 1361 is steaming now in the back of the shed, ready to go. Warren walks briskly down the tracks, looking back at her three, four times, as if for encouragement. Once outside, he turns around and gives Finney a wave, pulling up the hood of his windbreaker. Warren wanted to see her from the ground; he'll jump in once he sees how she's running. He is glad now; the view is better from here. She edges out of the shed and her jacket is gunmetal, gleaming, reflecting first the silver shed, then the gray-white sky. Steam spills from her sides, rolls into the waiting mist. Some have lamented the weather, how gloomy it is this morning. If this is gloomy, Warren thinks, gloom suits her. He has some second thoughts, looking at her in this queer light, about hitching his tool car, the Union Pacific "One Mile Down" to her—he'd thought the green would add nice color, but this morning she has a certain monochromatic dignity, like an old black and white photo, that he's not sure he wants to disturb. A darker car, maybe, would do better.

Finney looks down at him, blinks—or was it a wink? No, he blinks again, wipes his nose on his sleeve. A quiet man. He wouldn't sit in the engineer's seat until she had a full head of steam. These old guys, with all their secret charms and rituals, Weber with his father's oil can, Lloyd with his skip over the first rung, Junior with his lucky hat. Well, Warren has seen enough to know that luck plays its part.

Why this engine? Why spend half a million dollars trying to make her run, some have asked, when you could spread that out and keep twenty engines on display? She sat for thirty years. Every part on her was rusted or stripped or pitted or scarred. The guys down in Strasburg were almost hostile. But Warren, like all the guys on this crew, wanted to see her run, run full-out, hauling cars. Just once—then, of course, forever.

There are two K-4s left, out of a fleet of 425 engines. Strasburg has the other one. The rest were melted down for scrap after the war, when the diesels came in. When Warren was a boy—for he's one of the younger men on the crew, came into this as a mere fan—it was nothing to see a pair of K-4s or M-1s doubleheading, pulling a hundred, a hundred-and-fifty flat cars loaded with tanks. And passengers, too:

The K-4 pulled all the Pennsy's named trains—the Broadway Limited, Spirit of Saint Louis, Liberty Limited—she was the workhorse of the passenger fleet. Now she's—what? A *spectacle*, Warren thinks, watching her move slowly away from the shed. The coal that drives her, too. A couple of ghosts. This morning as he'd watched the men topping off the tender, he thought they were almost as excited to see the coal go to work as they were about the engine.

They leave in the dark under a steady rain, blearily attended by the Suburban's rusting wipers. As they near Bellefonte she sees cars parked along the road, up on the berm, hazards flashing, people gathered at crossings and on the overpasses. Her father finds an empty spot about ten miles out of town and pulls in behind three other cars.

Her grandfather is too agitated to sit, and not bothered by the rain. He stands with her father before the tracks, the two dressed alike in woolly flannel shirts and Timken vests, freebies from the shop. Her father reaches over, cups his hand under Pap's cigarette, then lights his own. He holds it backwards, tucked under his palm, a throwback to his Army days.

They stand there, backs to her, quietly talking. Steve climbs around on the bank, picking up stones and tossing them, following narrow trails through the weeds, whacking them with a stick. The rain has dwindled to a mist, but still the light is stifled, gray; it looks like dawn. Her grandfather's voice blends with the muted chatter of neighboring strangers sitting in folding chairs, blankets drawn around their shoulders, foam cups pressed to their chests.

They hear it, the faintest wail. Amy steps up, and a moment later her mother and Nanny join them, Nanny in a little cellophane rain bonnet, one of those things she can make appear out of her purse. The people line the tracks now, unconsciously leaning in, and then the train comes into sight.

When the whistle sounds, her grandfather straightens as if stung, and they all stare as it comes roaring down the track, a great cloud of smoke and steam blowing off to the left. Amy is surprised to feel tears well up, for what she can't even say; she knows nothing about trains. But it is so clearly a step out of time, and the sound of it is almost alive, the huffing of the engine just like a horse blowing on a long run, the raspy *hoo, whooo, hooo* of the whistle like the call of an owl or a mourning dove. It doesn't help that tears are sliding down her grandfather's face as he stands staring, welded to the cinders underfoot, that the handful of people who have gathered at this spot, like the thousands of others scattered along every mile of highway from here to Altoona, cry out and wave as the engine labors past. It's over in a moment; ashes flutter down around them along with the rain. The whistle blast warps and dies. The children ask as soon as the train disappears if it's time to go home; the adults frown, lingering to look down the empty track.

It's the first time she's ever seen tears in her grandfather's eyes. And he gives no words to it, but just blinks and stares, the strings in his neck flexing, and shoves the cinders a little with his foot before they follow the crowd back down to the road. Walking to the car, he stumbles in the ditch. Amy catches his arm and he mumbles, "Excuse me."

On the ride home, her mother keeps twisting around to talk to him from the front seat. "How about that, Daddy? That was something," she says. "Put on your seatbelt, Dad." But for once, he has nothing to say. She looks back every so often to see if he's fallen asleep. They wind through the narrow paths between the mountains, passing between the red walls of rock scarred by dynamite tracks, close, then falling away, then close again. Amy can see from his reflection in the windows, which comes and goes with the hills and the light, that he is not asleep.

That night she catches him in his room, kneeling by his bed, praying. She's surprised, not so much that he would pray, but that he would kneel to do it. That's when it strikes her: he really isn't all that big. He only wears a medium shirt.

Warren stands in the shop, once again after midnight. In the past week he's had about thirty hours of sleep, all in naps. He has developed one of the skills of the perennially exhausted, the ability to drop directly into dream sleep. Sometimes he wakes up after what feels like a visit to the far end of the universe, a full night's dreaming odyssey, and checking his watch realizes he was only out for twenty minutes.

She made the round trip without incident, breezed into Bellefonte to the cheers of a crowd bedecked, inexplicably, in Civil War regalia. Still, it has been a successful day. But as Warren packs, he moves more and more slowly, gathering his notebook and papers, replacing his toothbrush and razor in their proper slots in his ditty bag, collecting a week's accumulation of stuff to go back to his hotel for the first time in three days. He is tidy with his things. This isn't his shop. When the guys come back in the morning, he'd like it to be decent. But he's also prolonging the day because he knows that tomorrow, when he comes back to start packing up his equipment for the trip home to California, she will be just another train in the yard—a memorable one, a real beauty—but just a train.

WEATHER

His name is Charles Jenkins, but everyone calls him Zeke. No one in Little Bend, Zeke included, knows why. This is what people know about Zeke: when Zeke was fourteen, back when he was Charlie, he shot his brother Mark in a hunting accident. Everyone agreed they were too young to be out hunting alone, that Mark should have been wearing orange gear, that it never should have happened, but this is how it was: Zeke saw something, aimed his rifle and shot. He's been offering to die ever since, but death won't have him. He's a hundred thirty-five-pound Lazarus, wandering the streets of Little Bend day and night, in every kind of weather. Some people buy him beers or try to set him up with cable, fix his Schwinn when he wrecks it; others rob him when he's staggering home to his apartment from Smitty's or the Get Lucky. He can be surprisingly strong, and it is well known among the local police that he can inflict a nasty bite.

Little Bend is a river town, an old ferry station on the Susquehanna where people tend to stay, generation after generation. River rats, the people over in Tremont call them, but people who live along a river take things in stride. They are accustomed to emptying their basements when the waters start to rise. They keep their things in plastic tubs, run sumps. They tolerate the river's caprice, its seeming determination to be useless—rocky and shallow, unnavigable by boats of any consequence, treacherous to the hapless jet skiers and fishermen that come in their stead, with hidden ridges to run aground on and deep channels with sucking currents that swallow the wreckage. A good river to drown in, to build bridges over.

The day Zeke meets Lanie she looks like she's gardening, just the angle he can see of her, mostly behind, her arms reaching out to yank grass, a pile of pumpkins next to her. But she can't be growing pumpkins there, off the shoulder of Route 419. He gets closer and when she sits back, still on her knees, he can see she's clearing weeds from crosses, four white crosses in a row before her. She reaches into a paper sack next to her and pulls out a bunch of bright orange bows, lays them on the grass.

Zeke stands on the shoulder, not wanting to disturb her, takes a couple of sips from his paper cup of coffee. But he wonders about the crosses, so he steps through the weeds, into the grass. She glances back but keeps on with her work.

"Accident?" he finally says.

She nods, twisting wire around one of the crosses, straightening the bow. The last cross is smaller than the others.

"Who'd you lose?"

When she turns to look at him he can't tell if he's made her angry—you never know how people will take anything—but then she takes up the last bow, which has extra flowers and stuff on it, and what looks like a little note on yellow paper, and says, "My granddaughter. Amber. And my son."

"Sorry," Zeke says, a polite reflex.

She nods, starts moving pumpkins, settles one at the base of each cross. The last, smallest cross gets the smallest pumpkin. She wipes her upper lip, starts gathering her things.

"Hot, ain't," he says. It's late September and for two weeks it's been over eighty, humid but no rain. Like the weather got stuck. Even though the rest of the summer has been the opposite, wet and cool, windy. Killer hurricanes and floods, that tsunami. His friend Wilson says it's a sign of the end times, the weather gone crazy.

He wonders about the other crosses, but it seems like a bad question at the moment. In fact, he thinks he's probably used up his welcome. So he watches in silence as she finishes, puts her things in her paper sack, very tidy, and picks it up. He would offer to help but it's all air, he can tell, not heavy, and she's a sturdy sort. Not fat, not fat at all, just sturdy. A pretty grandma, he thinks. Lots of curly red-brown hair. He might have seen her around town.

"I think I know you," Zeke says, following her along the shoulder. "You drive a pink car?"

"Mary Kay," the woman says.

"Zeke," he says.

"No, I'm Lanie," she says. "It's a Mary Kay car."

"Oh, right," he says, having no idea what she's talking about. "I'm Zeke," he says again.

"I know who you are," Lanie says, but not mean—she gives him a friendly enough smile—smile down below, actually, but a frown around the eyes, like someone smiling into the sun, worried-looking.

"That any good?" she asks as he sips from his coffee.

"It's cold."

"But when it's hot, is it good? I've been meaning to try it."

"Well," Zeke says, looking up sideways. "Their regular coffee sort of tastes like tar, but the lattes are great."

"You drink lattes?" she says, and this time she smiles for real, almost laughs. It's a pretty sight. She stops, lifts her chin over the bag in her arms to check traffic. She's headed for the parking lot for Chiques Park. There he sees her pink car, poking out from behind a van.

"You never had a latte?" he says, and something about that makes her laugh again.

She walks to her car and he walks straight out of town, like he often does, though there's nothing on 419 out of town. Walks by the big church where Wilson goes. Down past the John Deere dealer. Steps over smashed rabbits and flattened cups and broken glass, all the stuff people fling out of their windows or run down. He walks a good mile out of town, mostly uphill, winding slowly up and north before crossing the road, looking left, right like Lanie did, and returning on the opposite shoulder, back down to Chiques Park. He sits at an overlook, a big square deck hanging on the edge of a cliff where you can sit at a picnic table or a bench and see Three Mile Island off to the north, the sparkle of the Susquehanna. Between, the woods.

Sometimes big hawks, hovering.

Coming back down the hill Zeke looks at Lanie's cross garden. You have to look hard; it's back almost in the trees, blocked by the guardrail. It looks good, he thinks. Real pretty like her car. Too bad there's no one out here to see.

Zeke sees her in line that week at Human Beans. She buys him a latte. After that, whenever he sees her around town, he says hello, waves at least.

The coffee shop is just down the block on the other side of the street from his apartment. For years Zeke lived in an old barn by the cemetery, wrapping himself in newspaper and baling plastic in cold weather, but three years ago some of the guys in town helped him fill out the forms and get set up with this place, right on the square. He doesn't like it because of the steps out front. Twice since he moved in he's fallen down them. The last time, he slipped on the ice, shattered a cheekbone and collapsed a lung, broke half his ribs on one side and was in intensive care for three days. The bill he received, which nobody will pay, exceeded the lifetime earnings figure, $38,000, on the little notices Social Security sends every year.

He's had two jobs in his life, mowing two different cemeteries.

One night in November, Zeke wakes at three a.m., the worst hour to wake, when everything's closed and no amount of beer or bourbon will put him out. He's tried sleeping pills but they only make matters worse—take one one night, it takes two the next, and if you try to cut back you're up for days—he wound up in the hospital once over that. Till he finally falls back to sleep he thinks it must be morning, and when he wakes again there's a gray light in his room that could mean any time, could mean night, even. His clock says seven and he's not sure which seven. He goes to the kitchen window and realizes it's morning; the sky's just dark and drizzling. He makes his way down to the coffee shop, shaky and confused, orders a double caramel latte "for here" and takes the giant mug they hand him over to a window seat. Some of the guys down at Smitty's give him a hard time about coming here, paying all that money to drink fancy coffees in this snooty place, but they never had a caramel latte. It's almost a meal. It's like food and dessert and coffee all in one drink. He can go half the day on one.

He's watching traffic, the rain clinging to the window when he's startled by Lanie sliding a plate in front of him. It has a biscuit on it almost as big as the plate, with eggs and ham and cheese in it, and big hunks of fruit around it.

"Eat," she says, and maybe it's her voice, or the hard look she's giving him, or maybe the smell of eggs and cantaloupe, which is making his stomach clench up, but

Zeke just manages to murmur, "Thanks," before she's heading off toward the door, a paper cup of coffee in her hand, all morning fresh and bright in her yellow slicker, her hair up in a fancy tie.

Zeke watches her step into the rain, pull up the hood of her slicker, waits until she's out of sight before pushing the plate back. He regrets coming out, leaving the house without washing up and shaving. He is usually particular about such things, tries to keep up a neat appearance. He tests his latte and it's ready to drink and he takes a big swallow, eyeing the sandwich. After the smell of the food has faded and he's gotten down enough of the latte, he breaks off some of the biscuit, and out of sheer determination not to waste Lanie's present he manages to eat half.

That weekend she passes him on the hill up 419. When he reaches the top he sees her over by the guardrail, tending her crosses. She's taking off little bunches of Indian corn she must have fixed to them for Thanksgiving, piling up colorful gourds in the grass next to her. It's almost December and still unseasonably warm, not even coat weather yet, all but seventy degrees.

He gives her a chance to see him, stands close enough so she can't miss him. Finally she glances back, looks him over, says, "You're looking better," like she's sort of glad about it.

He walks closer, stands next to her while she takes a bunch of fancy wreaths out of a paper sack, wreaths with a good piney smell, with big red bows. Lanie loops them over the crosses, adjusts the branches. Pulls from the bag a small but heavy-looking box with shiny gold wrapping and a red bow.

"Who're the other two for?" Zeke asks.

She puts the present at the base of the littlest cross, only twelve or so inchés high, fluffs up the ribbon.

"A young couple, a nurse and her husband. He was bringing her home from work, out at the VA hospital."

She packs up the gourds and Zeke takes the bag—no reason he shouldn't help—and Lanie doesn't object, lets him walk with her back to the road.

"My son—"

They check traffic, cross.

"Justin. He was high on meth, drunk, too. He crossed into their lane. The police said he was going about ninety-five."

Zeke drops back, just a half step, gives her the lead. He stands by while she deposits her things in the trunk, takes out her purse. He props the bag of gourds against the side of the trunk so it won't fall over, folds the top over several times and scrunches it tight, like he's trying to contain a live animal instead of a bunch of gourds. She mumbles thanks and closes the trunk and stands there, hand on the lid, keys splayed out against the metal, looking at some people flying kites at the overlook. She looks tired, Zeke thinks, not like the other morning, and she's not making any move toward the car door, so he says, "You ever look at the view from up here?" and she says it's been a long time.

He leads her across the field, past a boy who is running, head down, a kite jumping in the grass behind him, somebody directing him, slow down, put your arm up, hold it up high. They sit on a bench built into the side of the deck, to the left of a large sign showing all the birds you can see up here. From their seat they can see the view and the kite flyers. The little kid is still running back and forth, dragging his kite behind him. Lanie smiles, just with her mouth.

She tells him about the accident, what her son did. Ran four lights in town before coming up here and wrecking into that couple. Had the cops after him at the end. "What I don't understand," she says, not looking at him, never taking her eyes off the kites, or maybe the people, "is why Amber stayed in the car. He stopped at his girlfriend's house on the way out, and he was there at least fifteen, twenty minutes. So she was in the car that whole time, long enough for him—well, anyway. She had time to get out of the car. And she must have known he was not okay to drive with by then—she knew what to do; her mother and I both talked to her about it. If her Dad got like that she was supposed to leave him, no matter what, no matter where they were, she was supposed to leave him and have somebody call her mom or call me. So why would she stay in the car?"

Zeke says nothing. He heard something about that wreck. Cars on fire, all the fire trucks came out, all the cops, everybody. One of those nights where every siren in town was going.

"Unless she was asleep. It was eleven. She could have been asleep."

A man is running behind the boy now, holding the kite high, calling out instructions. He launches it; the kite floats for a moment, rises as the boy yanks the string as he's told, then takes a quick turn and falls straight down. Lanie is looking through them.

"But she couldn't have slept through the sirens. She couldn't have slept through the whole thing."

She tells him about her daughter-in-law, who moved back to Texas afterward, taking Lanie's only other grandchild, Devon, with her. Not that she could blame her, she says. About her older son who lives in Chicago and has no children yet, and who gave up on Justin and River Bend and maybe Lanie and her husband, too, about ten years ago.

"It's true what they say," Lanie tells him. "A son is your son till he says 'I do,' but a daughter's your daughter her whole life through."

Zeke, who knows very little about mothers and sons and daughters and mothers, nods.

"What are the white trees?" he asks her. They come out at Halloween when the leaves die, their white branches just like antlers or bone.

"Sycamores, I think," Lanie says, finally turning her head, looking down at them. When the cold comes, it comes in a day, and like something out of Siberia. No snow, no real weather, no ice, just everything like iron and so cold it makes your eyes ache. Zeke spends a lot of time indoors, logs a lot of careless hours at Smitty's. He's come almost to prefer Lanie time. He gets lattes "for here" and sometimes adds a muffin. He waits by the window, and a couple of times when she comes in she sits there with him, looking at the paper, the magazines. Lanie says she's retired. She doesn't do shows, she says, doesn't sell makeup anymore except to a handful of ladies who still call for it. Her husband is retired, too, in more ways than one, Zeke thinks, since he doesn't seem to talk to Lanie much, otherwise why would she be telling this stuff to him? But he would never say that to Lanie. He suspects it's different for her when he listens, just like talking to Lanie is nothing like talking to the guys down at Smitty's.

At Christmas she buys him a little tree with built-in lights. She says he should put it in his window, and he does, setting it on top of an end table next to his television set. Lanie thinks everyone should have a Christmas tree. After New Year's Lanie tells him take it down, it's time, and he packs it away as neatly as it came, the balls in their special slots, the tree folding down just like an umbrella and breaking in two, nesting into a surprisingly small box. He puts the boxes in his hall closet, all together in the corner for next year.

She takes him here and there in her pink car, over to the K-Mart in Tremont when he needs things. One night in February, after a week of sunshine and sixty degrees, they get caught in a freak thunderstorm of snow. They're in the K-Mart buying toilet paper and shampoo and toothpaste, valentines for her grandson in Texas, a pair of shoes for Zeke, and they come out of the store to find two inches of snow fell while they were shopping. They have a hard time pushing the cart to her car, the snow is falling so thick and fast, and Lanie starts down the road toward Little Bend but has to pull over. When the lightning strikes it's like a camera flash right in their eyes, and then after, for whole seconds, they can't see, and they sit there turning their heads side to side and blinking, and the sky is unreal, lit upside down or something, and Zeke begins to think maybe Wilson is right, this could be it, time to throw himself flat on the ground and start confessing, and God will come stand over him and say take your time, Zeke, I got all the time in the world.

"Were they calling for this?" Lanie asks. Zeke doesn't think so.

When spring comes—and it comes in fits and spurts, a hot spell followed by an ice storm, hail once, sudden downpours—he sometimes walks to her house, a nice brick place on the old main street of town, near the watch factory. She has bunchy lace curtains and those little lights in the windows, a porch with twinkly white lights and wooden chairs and a swing. It's a perfect house, Zeke thinks, what a house should be, like a house in a book or a picture. Sometimes if he's in the neighborhood late he comes and sits on her swing. It squeaks, so he doesn't swing hard. Once, he wakes up there just before dawn and doesn't remember coming at all. He finds his bike by the steps and rides home, accompanied for a short while by an old gray cat he calls Howler.

Zeke used to ride his bike everywhere. He was headed for a job interview over in Tremont thirty years ago, but he stopped in at Smitty's beforehand. So the joke goes, "How long's it take to get to Tremont, Zeke?" and Zeke says, "I'm gettin' there, babe, I'm gettin' there."

But how Zeke loves to be sober. He tries to stretch it out later and later that spring as the days grow long again, when he's feeling up to it. When he's feeling really good he holds out half the day, will start off early with a caramel latte to go, carry it with him up and down the streets and alleys of Little Bend, feel the last traces of alcohol sweating out through his pores. If he can make it till four, five in the afternoon, that first beer tastes like The First, like the only beer you've ever had. It tastes like the one you keep trying to drink long after the first one, when your mouth turns to tin and people become assholes and it's not really fun anymore.

One day he comes to find Lanie out in her front yard, standing on a stepladder, working a sledgehammer, driving a big wooden cross into the ground. She can't exactly swing the hammer, but she's not just dropping it, either. She's giving it her all, and the look on her face as she pounds makes Zeke hang back. She takes out some purple fabric, finally sees him there by the neighbor's fence.

"Is it going to rain or not?" she asks him, almost accusingly. She drapes the fabric around the cross like a scarf, then gets a bouquet out of a see-through tub and ties it around the middle.

She brings beautiful flowers for her roadside crosses, mint-colored puffy bows, a basket full of brightly colored plastic eggs to put by the smallest one. Her gold present was gone when they got there, and Zeke asks her what was in it, and she says just a note, and a rock to keep it from blowing away, so whoever took it is in for a letdown.

"My mom always said, you love your kids, Lanie, that's all you can do, that's all they need," she tells him. "You'll worry yourself to death over all these little things and someday you'll realize you loved them, that's all you had to do."

Zeke takes a sip of his latte, still burning hot, winces. "But all her kids turned out fine. So of course she could afford to think that."

He nods, blows through the little hole in the lid, riffling the foam.

"But I treated them both the same; that's what I don't understand. They were both so different, but I loved them both exactly the same. I might have spoiled Justin a little— he was younger, and never as good at school, or sports. So, yeah, I might have babied him. Maybe I babied him too much," she says, and her voice grows tight, tough Lanie starting to blink.

"It's just like anything else, Lanie. It ain't no magic power."

"What?"

"Love," Zeke says. "It's just another thing that ain't enough."

One snowfall on the crocuses, one hard freeze to the daffodils. The magnolias bud, as always, too soon, and litter the ground with soggy petals. The river that could never carry much goes on with its make-work, wearing away at the rock that forms its bed.

"Is spring ever coming?" Lanie asks.

This is what Zeke hates: when he doesn't drink enough and he wakes up in the middle of the night and he can't shake his dream.

It's always the same. He goes into Smitty's and he's been there drinking and he looks up and there's Mark, sitting next to him at the bar. And Zeke says, "Mark?" And Mark says, "I'm fine, Charlie, I'm fine." And Zeke feels his arm, and it's real, and he's so happy he orders Coors seven-ouncers and tells the bartender to keep them coming, and they sit there and drink and talk old times. Then Mark turns to him, and Zeke can see that his right eye is a hole, a tiny hole like a cigarette burn in a shirt, and Zeke starts to cry, but Mark says, "No, Charlie, I'm fine. Look, it doesn't even hurt. Here, feel." And he takes Zeke's finger and puts it in the little hole and it goes right through, because the back of his head is missing, but he's saying, "See, Charlie? You missed. You didn't even come close."

$0 = 1$

My questions never shocked you, my appeals to fact. You never ran crying from the room or shunned me when I called out your father, your book. I was surprised at first. You even laughed once and put your hand on my knee, *Oh, Claire!*

Sacrifice is senseless, I argued, imputation is illogical. Why must you wear that cover on your head? You had answers for everything. Fear is the beginning of understanding, you said. The blood of the lamb will wash you white as snow. No, I said, sorry, no. Your math was maddening. But I had to give you this: you were the only one in the family who would talk to me, who didn't walk away.

When you got sick, the family prayed. I read all I could. There were tested and untested therapies; you tried some of each. A cancer cell, I learned, is one that has forgotten how to die, a tiny flipped switch. OFF/ON, LOW/HIGH, the primitive language of ASCII. I sent you books and articles, passages highlighted. Shark cartilage. *T-cells—A new therapy—available in Mexico but worth checking?* That was more than a decade ago. I scarcely remember now. Actually, I remember you; I do not recall myself.

Once, they held a special service for you, a laying on of hands. I was surprised when they asked me to come up front and join them. I sat with my hand resting uneasily on your thigh, feeling your heat through the thin layers of dress and slip and pantyhose, and did my best to pray. I wasn't in a position to ask for any favors, so I just clenched my eyes shut and thought dear God don't whammy her because of my hand. Such was my faith, then and now, sufficient to see me roasted, to call down the fires of hell. Never over that hump to the graceful place where you lived, Ruth.

For a while, you got better. Sick or well, you never changed. When your hair fell out, you wore a wig and a handkerchief; you replaced your breasts with a prosthetic bra. You left your skin, which was often inflamed, uncovered. You were unretouched. If any of these things troubled you, if you had any instinct to vanity, you kept it to yourself. Talk about you inevitably turned into talk about me, or whoever else was in the room, or the children you taught, or Jesus.

In 2004, Stephen Hawking scared all the scientists who were smart enough to understand (which wasn't a large population, but still) when he suggested that a black hole might be powerful enough to eat information. He announced this to a crowd accustomed to running the math on doom, measuring out the life span of the sun, laying bets on whether the universe would go out with a bang or just scatter and go cold—none of this perturbed them. But the loss of information itself, an empty little maw that could make three no longer three—this was more than they could bear, and they revolted.

Why would anyone make something, I once argued, only to throw it away? Love gives up nothing willingly. But you said no, no. Love exacts a heavy price. Love gives up everything willingly.

When Anna called, I didn't quite believe it. They'd said you were dying so many times before, and I was young and didn't really believe in death, not a death you sit politely waiting out. So I took my time, cutting asters from my yard, wrapping the stems in wet paper towels and bagging them for the trip, tying them with a yellow ribbon, propping them carefully on the car seat. No wonder you thought you were dying—they were always telling you it was the end. What else did they ever think about? I had seen you only a couple of weeks before at Anna's, where you were staying. You looked tired, but you said you were feeling better. This much I remember clearly: you were sitting on the sofa, pictures and cards from the children, some of the hundred or more people who loved you, scattered on the table before you. Trust and obey, one read. Miss Ruth Get Well. In them, you appeared as a pot-bellied stick figure with hands like tiny suns, a purple-haired superhero sailing through the clouds. Suddenly you said, with a determination that seemed almost like anger, "I just keep holding on to his promises, knowing that he never fails," and you held your hands out as if you were holding onto the rung of a ladder, doing a chin-up. For once, I said nothing, although I could not stop myself from thinking it: holding onto thin air. Swell.

Cars were pulled up onto Anna's lawn, parked end to end. I found an open spot by the wash line and came in through the back entrance, adding my shoes to a heap in the breezeway. I heard them, their muffled singing coming through the ceiling, growing louder when I opened the door to the kitchen. Rapid, sock-footed steps sounded on the stairs and Anna appeared. I gave her the asters in their soggy bag and she laid them on the counter without looking and said, *Go up, go on up,* and actually gave me a push. The stairs were narrow and steep, with a tiny landing midway where someone had placed a battery-operated candle and a flower arrangement bearing a tiny card. So funereal, I thought. So morbid.

Are you prepared? the old man was forever asking in his Old World accent, *Are you prepared?*

They were packed into a little attic room, wooden folding chairs crammed into rows, singing from hymnals. You lay before them on a hospital bed, your eyes sweeping back and forth, restless with pain, your arm propped on a pillow, big around as a grapefruit at the elbow, barely recognizable as an arm anymore. They made room for me and I moved forward, touched your shoulder where it looked like it wouldn't hurt. I whispered in your ear and kissed your cheek. It was sticky and hot. A pause, a number was called, pages turned. I backed slowly through the crowd, back the way I'd come. I didn't know any hymns and I didn't want to watch you die. Downstairs, I sat on Anna's couch. Across the road, some distance away, a tiny tractor plowed. That afternoon the well ran dry; a fire truck came to fill it. I watched the oldest brother dump a bottle of bleach in the trap, talk with the firefighters, hold out some money. The firemen waved it away. Once Anna came downstairs, walked briskly across the kitchen, picked up a dishtowel and pressed it to her face. She cried quietly into it for a minute, then laid it back down on the countertop and smoothed it flat, staring out the window over the sink. After a few minutes she went back upstairs.

Toward evening, the singing stopped. There was a quiet commotion, voices rising and falling, chairs groaning. Later the funeral director rolled you out on a stretcher, zipped up in a black bag like the ones dry cleaners use to cover an expensive coat.

Schrodinger is frequently misapplied. *From the position of the cat*, he said all along, *there is no contradiction.*

More than 300 people came to your homegoing service, so many they had to bring up folding chairs from the basement. I could not help but wonder how many people my funeral would draw. A number less than or equal to 300, certainly. Likely smaller by an order of 10. The old man went to the front of the church and said, *I don't understand.*

Bad news: a logic gate requires two posited contradictory states that are not themselves subject to logic. UP/DOWN. 0/1. Information is a construct.

They sang for more than an hour. They sang without accompaniment, slowly and carefully in complicated harmony, as if the singing itself mattered. There were so many people there, so many voices familiar with the music, that even as they walked out of the church and across the driveway to the gravesite, falling in behind the brothers who carried you on their shoulders, the song never died out, but just broke up and meandered a little on the stairs. *Happy day*, they sang, *happy day.* Anna's husband had made the casket, a plain, hand-rubbed walnut box—no handles, no rails, no silly doorknockers or trim. They lowered you into the grave with ropes and took turns throwing in dirt. I rolled and unrolled my program, ready to go. But at the point in a funeral when everyone usually leaves, they stayed. The brothers took up more shovels and started piling damp dirt into the grave, wrestling the rocky clay into the hole, and I realized they were going to fill it. Several times Daniel, the youngest, jumped into the hole. He stomped and chopped the dirt with the shovel so it wouldn't settle later, rubbing tears away with his sleeve. They sang until the hole was filled and leveled and tamped smooth, ready for seed; I mouthed the words the best I could and worried my program into felt. Only the children strayed, running off to the playground behind the church, working up an appetite for the lunch they knew would follow.

There was a time I've never told anyone about, many years before I came here, when I went skating alone on a lake, following the edge of a large clearing someone else had swept clean. I'd borrowed the skates and was unsure of the ice. In places it seemed frozen to maybe a foot deep, the ice bubbly and white and gnarled and choppy, but in others it was slick and black and fast. I tested it, listening to the tiny snapping sounds of the ice, here and there a deeper creak, and decided it was all right, the sounds harmless as a house settling. I skated farther and farther into the perfect snow, carving out lines and circles and arcs legible only to the wavering stars, until it was so dark and I was so far out that the click and slide of the skates seemed like the only thing left—no lake, no trees, no skater. Just a sound that was quieter than silence.

The new religion is just like the old, running primitive end games around the intractable zero sum. 0/1.

Through the singing, on and on, I heard Daniel's blade, the patient clank and scrape of the metal on stone. It was the sound of being suspended, of being carried on someone's shoulders, of old leaves riffling and inscrutable figures being carved on a blank page. It was a sound I know too well, Ruth—the sound of being alone.

HALF BEAT

We stayed always in the wooden chairs, eyes on the carpet, even though after half an hour it made our rears itch and our legs ache. It wasn't like we'd never seen a bug before, but the roaches there were sizeable and fast, and the fabrics on the sinking sofa and armchairs, with their complicated tangles of brown foliage, seemed murky and threatening. The sofa had black head shadows on the back, hand shadows on the arms, innumerable blossoming stains on the seats and three great butt dents. No kid in her right mind would sit in such a thing, though the adults often did. Adults would pretend such a thing was okay. They're great pretenders, actually.

Sometimes when we couldn't sit any longer, when we felt like there were firecrackers going off in our legs, we'd step cautiously over to the big windows at the front of the room and watch the people out on the street, or climb the stairs, stepping down to the entrance, back up to the second-floor waiting room, up the next flight—*quietly*—to the studio hall, back down to the waiting room.

The Mozart Conservatory of Music sat in a neon part of Toledo—sad neon, daytime neon. At some time maybe it had

been more, maybe not. There was no telling, really. You can't
exactly ask someone, was this place always this way or was it
nice once? Certainly Miss Wood had real credentials: Juilliard,
1933. We knew this from the brochure; it was the reason my
father brought us all the way in from Promontory every Saturday
morning. We also knew instinctively to pretend the cockroaches
didn't exist when any of the adults were around, even our father.
Especially our father. Just as we ignored the messages through
the front windows on the marquee of the Esquire XXX burlesque
across the street, which was always advertising Live Girls Live
Girls. Madame Renault, Miss Wood's partner, who had a theater
background, called it "the dance hall." That always made Miss
Wood roll her eyes. Miss Wood was no-nonsense.

My father explained to us one morning the subtle
difference between a burlesque hall and a strip club, the
former implying at least a certain level of artistic integrity.
He saw art everywhere, or he wanted to, especially in old
things. Maybe only in old things. He'd taken a wicked
glee the fall before from the fact that Jimmy Carter's
campaign bus had to park out there because the
Democratic Party headquarters were on the same block.
The TV crews had to get creative to shoot the bus from
an angle that didn't show XXX Live Girls over Mr. Carter's
head. Riding home from school on the bus that fall, the
handful of kids whose parents were Democrats would
chant, "Carter, Carter," and we would shout them down
with "Peanut farmer!" as if that settled matters somehow.
Which was funny, because the richest, most influential
people in Promontory were the farmers. But I guess a
soybean, to our way of thinking, had an inherent dignity
that a peanut lacked, and the fact that this guy talked about
his peanuts, about their nutritive qualities and how
valuable they might prove against world hunger, made it
downright comical. We hooted and clutched our sides,

shoved one another into the aisles. A peanut farmer, president of the United States.

So, you never know.

Madame Renault, with her Broadway background, permitted—possibly even encouraged—singing through the nose. That's why my father had us wait for Miss Wood. Madame Renault had not seen a live performance in several decades, but she still wore stage makeup. She plucked her eyebrows all the way out and drew them back in—two fierce black arcs—a full inch higher than they had ever been, so she always looked a little shocked. She was ballerina thin and wore heavy black-heeled dancing shoes, and would clap and stomp in a way that made her limbs look bojangly and loose, like she might come apart if it weren't for the hard strings that held her together. During my lessons, her students' yowling show tunes and her stomping along would come through the walls, only slightly muffled, and Miss Wood would press her eyes shut and breathe, like she was trying to block her out, or maybe fighting a headache.

Miss Wood had long, steely hair that she wound into a bun, and she wore muslin dresses with faded flowers and buttons up to the neck, her full slips visible through the worn cotton, peeping out from her hem. She spoke softly, deliberately, but if you missed enough notes she would take your finger and bang it on the key—that's A, A, A. Sometimes she would get so frustrated with me she'd just give up and play. She'd be talking and picking something out on the keys, illustrating some point, and then her hands would take off, crawling blindly, effortlessly up and down the keyboard with their spidery, knowing grace, and you could almost see the music going to waste, pouring down the grimy hallway and out into Toledo, spilling over into the shoe outlet next door, over the heads of the sad people with canes who moved silently through toppling chimneys of odd lots, double-E wides, double-A narrows, sandals in winter, boots in summer.

One morning she came to a lull in the music and stopped, her eyes straight ahead, looking through the wall like she saw it, too. Disappearing down the hall. Her left hand dropped; the right poised over the keys, lilting, ready to continue. This was the time, I'd learned, when I could hit her with a question.

"What was his name?" I asked.

"Who?" Miss Wood said, her head slowly coming down, her right wrist dropping.

"You said you had a suitor once."

"Oh," she said, her eyebrows gathering. "That was Mr. Treski. Louis."

"Did he ask you to get married?"

She looked over at me, a little sharply. "He did. But my mother did not approve." Madame Renault had told my father that much two months ago, in a moment of spite.

"How come?"

"Because he was a butcher. And he was Polish, and Catholic." Her mouth closed decisively. She retrieved her pencil, always freshly sharpened, from the tray, and added, "It was a different time." She brought the book to her lap and began writing instructions on the page in her tremulous scrawl, the pencil scraping against the nubby paper. Her face was downy and pale, softened into uncertain curves, or maybe only looked that way because her eyes were dark brown and watchful and sharp. Her chest rose and fell with her breathing; her heartbeat set her buttons trembling ever so faintly over her chest, at her throat.

Then, next door, stomp stomp stomp *Ma, he's making eyes at me, Ma, he's awful nice to me . . .*

Miss Wood frowned, gave her head a shake. "For next week, I want you to start on 'Barcarolle.' And continue to play through 'Etude.'" Then she got out her little star box, even though I'd flubbed "Etude" in two places. She picked out a green star, lifted it to her tongue and pressed it, fishtailing, to the page until it was fixed in place.

My little brother, John, always took his lesson first, since he couldn't sit in the waiting room for long. When he was done, my father would take him to an antique auction two blocks south, while Ellen and I took voice and piano. That day they came back a little early, during Ellen's voice lesson. My father was toting a long black case, huffing from the stairs, sweating even though it was September and already cold. "You won't believe this," he said. "An alto sax. Two bucks." He set the scuffed, dusty case on the sofa and popped the latches. Inside, nested in black velvet, the sax was intricate, gleaming, with the impressiveness that all instruments have, the gravity of a fine thing. He screwed it together, narrating—we'll get a new mouthpiece, some scratches here, they can refinish that—then held it out, triumphant, weighed it in one arm. "Here, try it out," he said, passing it to me.

"Daddy," John protested, and my father soothed him, "You're next, you're next," while I worked my hands around it, found places for them. It was unwieldy, heavy in my arms but also soothing to hold, the worn brass warming instantly to my skin, the keys cupping my fingertips. I pushed, and the valves made a satisfying *puh puh puh* sound, like tiny mouths opening and closing.

I passed it carefully to John while my father instructed him: left hand here, right hand here—*don't!*—put your mouth on the mouthpiece! Just pretend, Johnny, just pretend. I took my hands away. They smelled bitter, like pennies.

I knew better than to ask my father what he intended to do with it, who would play it. I knew it would wind up in one of the unused rooms upstairs in our house. He just couldn't bear to see an instrument go without a bid, to see it tossed in a variety box or sent to the dump. The summer before, my father had taken voice lessons from Miss Wood, too, to prepare for an open try-out for the opera chorus. We kept it a secret from my mother until after they turned him down—he had a nice voice, they told him, but too limited a range. At the time I thought it was just a secret for fun, like a birthday surprise, but now that I've reached the age that he was then, I think it was just too big to share, too embarrassing, that for a little while he'd had the nerve to harbor a dream of music for himself.

The opera in Toledo was good, drawing big names like Giorgio Tozzi, Martina Arroyo, and almost Richard Tucker. Almost because, sadly, Tucker died the week before he was due to perform. My father had been stunned. "What some people will do to get out of going to Toledo," he would joke years later, after he'd gotten over it enough to inject a little humor, although it still choked him up sometimes just to think of it, how close he'd come to witnessing greatness.

For me, the opera was sheer spectacle—laughing Musetta riding onstage in a carriage hauled by a real white horse, live camels in *Aida*. They could make the sun set or the moon rise so imperceptibly and magically you didn't even notice it happening, and once they even made it snow—the stage was glowing, a vibrant blue, then the snow began to fall flake by flake, just like a real storm, then heavier and heavier, and the singers left real snowtracks as they wandered the stage, hugging themselves against the cold.

So I understood why my father wanted to join them on that magnificent stage with its sweeping two-story curtains, its outsize scenery, why he wanted to be one of those enchanted people, the men with their round-arm claps on the back, their elaborate courtesies during curtain calls— *after you—after you*—the towering bass always going last, the ladies who collapsed between them, sinking into their beautiful gowns, hands to their hearts, then pressed to their lips, while people shouted and threw roses. They were even grander after the performances, those elegant people. Of course my father wanted to be among them. They hailed from another, more beautiful place.

Every week after our lessons, Ellen and I met my best friend Genevieve under an old oak tree at the back of my neighbor's empty lot, where I filled them in on the mystery of Miss Wood's lost love. "What's wrong with being a butcher?" Ellen asked after I relayed my latest findings. Her hair blew across her face and she reached up to untangle it from her glasses. Behind us the cornstalks, tan and brittle, clattered in the field. Genevieve pulled her jacket closed, crossed her arms over her knees.

"That's just it," I said. "Just because he was a butcher? Or Catholic? Or what? It doesn't add up."

"There's more to it," Ellen said, squinting.

"Of course there is," Genevieve said.

"I'll find out," I said. "She's warming up to me."

The oak tree was one of our hideouts. It was a lone oak standing between our neighborhood and the fields beyond, so old that when the three of us pressed ourselves against the trunk and stretched out our arms, our fingers barely touched. The neighbors kept the lot empty and mowed and untreated, as people did then, so it was a full acre of ground with nothing better to do than breed clover and dandelion, and draw bees that we caught in jars during the summer.

"Come on," Genevieve said, standing up. "Let's go." She zipped up her jacket and I followed her without another word, because I followed Genevieve everywhere. She was my better half—bigger, older, stronger, smarter. We were blood sisters, spit sisters, co-founders of a dog club, had read in tandem through the entire juvenile and young adult sections of the Promontory Public Library and were now dabbling in adult fantasy, Bradbury and Tolkien and Hesse. We caught snakes together on the railroad tracks, bringing them triumphantly back to the neighborhood in coffee cans, eager to show that we were not afraid. She ducked into one of the rows of corn, hands overhead like a diver, and I stepped in behind, followed by Ellen, who was allowed to tag along, it was understood, only when we felt like it. I kept my head down, brushing the leaves aside, following Genevieve's sneakers down the rows toward the railroad tracks.

Promontory was named after a thirty-foot bank of land, the abandoned shore of an old course of the Maumee River, which had since moved farther north. The river meandered through a great flat plain that had been washed for millennia by floodwaters from Lake Erie, and so you could dig down two, three feet and turn over nothing but rich, loamy black soil just like the potting soil you buy in bags. In spring, the soil sprouted everywhere orderly rows of soybeans and corn, in neat square plots stretching from horizon to horizon, with occasional clumps of trees clustered between the fields like lonely shepherds. As summer came on, the horizon pulled a disappearing act, as the plants rose up to and then higher than the cars, so by mid-summer, it was corn and sky. Corn, soybeans and sky.

I remember the house always first as a ghost, an image from an old photo on glossy paper, fading as the paper slowly lost its magic chemical properties. The photo was passed down from owner to owner, handed to my parents along with the closing papers. Because I was seven when we moved in, I can never be sure how much of my early memory of that gray house is real and how much derives from that milky old picture. If you looked closely at the photo, you could see a few strands of ivy fingering up from the foundation. When we moved in, the house was half green with it. The leaves made a slapping noise in the wind. Underneath the ivy, the walls were covered with gray stucco sculpted into cruel points. If you got too close, those walls drew blood. You had to be careful when you were down there nosing around under the bushes, smelling the dirt and the mystery bulbs and the deadly things that grew there, lilies of the valley, jack in the pulpit, pokeweed, nightshade.

My parents were restoring the house, which was perched on Promontory's single bank. When it was built, it overlooked a canal. When we lived there, it presided over a limited access highway. The back part of the second floor was a maze of new studs and plywood, while the front rooms upstairs were nearly untouched. The downstairs was a hodgepodge of repairs: cracked, water-stained plaster walls with bands of overlapping brown wallpaper where a drop ceiling had been, plywood patches in the floors. Doors opened onto nothing; holes in the walls and the ceilings were duct-taped shut with sheets of black plastic, which sagged under the weight of crumbling plaster.

The property had been abandoned for some years before we bought it, and neglected for more, and it bore fruit of some earlier time, things nobody grew anymore: earnest catalpa trees with insane sticky bean pods as long as your arm, inedible currants, musky blue concord grapes, tiger lilies, spearmint, violets, hollyhock. Every limb or shrub or tree or weed in the yard bore something. We uncovered an ugly purple mound of leaves: the following summer we had a bathtub full of rhubarb. One afternoon, in a fit of pioneer zeal, my father tilled a sixty-foot-square garden and, being inexperienced at gardening, planted one hundred tomato plants. We had tomato wars with the neighborhood kids that summer; my mother took up canning. We were relieved when frost came and the plants finally quit. It was as if the ground were claiming us, and not the other way around. At least, it seemed that way to me.

"You must master the metronome before you may abandon it," Miss Wood would say. "That is the difference between improvisation and incompetence."

"But I can't—keep time," I'd plead, "with it ticking. I hear the ticking, I lose the time."

"Practice," Miss Wood would say sternly, and for a moment it was as if she could see me running around the yard, hiding under bushes, lying upside down on the sofa staring at the dust motes in the light rather than practicing. "Just like the notes, Claire. You keep your eyes on them, read them each time, and eventually the letters go away."

I couldn't sight read yet either. "I keep time better without it," I pouted.

"That is how I learned," Miss Wood said, which was a pretty good closing argument. But I hated even the look of that thing, and whenever Miss Wood turned it on I lost my place, found myself staring up at it, hands paralyzed, neurons misfiring, chaos. The very shape of it was offensive, its tiny stupid head, the tocker waggling back and forth like a finger, *tsk tsk tsk.*

I limped through my piece, restarting once, twice, a third time. The metronome droned on, tripping me up, and then Miss Wood's hands came down. "Pathetique," the second movement, pastoral and sweet. I could hear her point, the dutiful innocence of the left hand, which marched along, predictable, a steady four beats, while the right hand offered over it a melody, wandering, uncertain, sad. "Hear it?" Miss Wood said, meaning the even tempo of the left, and I nodded. But I also knew that it was all the places where Miss Wood strayed, where she doubled up or hesitated on the right, that made the piece hers, that made it worth hearing. You didn't have to be good or even musically inclined to see that. You could see it in her hand, the way she'd reach for the next note and then draw up before striking, the way her lips would part so slightly, or her eyebrows lift, when she pulled these little tricks.

"Miss Wood?" I said when she had stalled, had fallen into gazing, the strings still humming, the metronome mindlessly wagging.

"Do you see?" Miss Wood said, still staring ahead.

I nodded.

"How did you meet him? Mr. Treski."

She leaned forward, stopped the metronome.

"That was a long time ago," she said, pulling down my book, reaching for her pencil.

"You don't remember?"

She blinked at me. I looked quickly down at the piano pedals. She wrote a few words in the book, underlined them. "His father used to make deliveries to our house," she said, "Tuesdays and Saturdays at eight o'clock. One morning, Louis came for the delivery. I was practicing, and I turned and saw him standing in the doorway, listening. After that, we spoke every morning when he came. Only during deliveries—he never called at our house."

"That's all you did? Talk in your living room?"

"Once I visited him at market. My mother had to travel to Detroit to sign some papers after her uncle died. And when Louis asked, I decided to go ahead and see him. But Toledo was not the big city then that it is today, and our neighborhood being what it was, my mother heard about it the moment she came back. She was quite angry. That's when Louis asked me to marry him."

"So what happened?"

"My mother wouldn't hear of it. I was off to Juilliard anyway. She said that time would resolve it, and it did. When I came back from school, he had married a girl from River Park."

I weighed this.

"But you turned him down, right? Before you went away?"

"I told him it was impossible."

"But—would you have married him when you came back, if he hadn't married someone else?"

"It was not an issue," Miss Wood said. "He was married then."

The front windows in our house were original, with wavy glass that made it look rainy when it wasn't. When we were smaller, when we first moved in, Ellen and I would go upstairs in our underwear and scramble around over the boxes and make elaborate forts. We had boxes up there from as far back as Indiana, where I was born—United, Allied, Atlas, Stevens. McCormick Mayflower had the best boxes, with green clipper ships on them.

From the road, I always thought those windows out front looked like eyes.

In Promontory I knew all the neighborhood lore, the teenage exploits and the father follies, how it always rained after Kevin Kirby washed his sports car, the time Genevieve's Dad erected a snow fence on the wrong side of his driveway, and wound up with a big naked green space in the yard and a ten-foot drift the length of his driveway that hung around to torment him through April. I knew all the secrets of the place, which trees were the good climbers and where the best seats were. How my neighbor's pears were best after they fell, scooped up from an early snow on the way to the bus stop, when they were so ripe I would

press the waxy skin to my mouth and the pear would rush
in, icy wet and sweet, and the juice would run down to my
wrist. I'd hear shouting and then I'd run, bangs freezing to
my forehead, fringe from my suede purse slapping
awkwardly against my leg, chuck the half-pear over the
bank, give my hands a hasty snow wash, pull myself up onto
the bus steps, slipping on the dirty slush.

The following week, I put in a respectable performance, one
that seemed to hearten Miss Wood. She pulled the book into
her lap, and while she turned the pages back to the start of
the piece and reached up for her pencil, I asked, as casually
as I could, "So whatever happened to Mr. Treski? After you
came back from college, did you ever see him again?"

She tilted up her chin, then looked back down at the book,
and I wasn't sure she'd heard me until she said, "Yes and
no." She carefully drew a star on the page, something she
did when she was particularly pleased, and wrote some words
next to it, then put the pencil down. Her penciled stars always
had a tiny loop in each turn. "When I came back from school,
he was still making deliveries. He used to come in the back
door and put the meat in the icebox for us and leave the bill
on the table. I would see his truck pull up in the alley while I
was practicing, and then I would see him go again. But after
my mother died—she died in '47—I noticed one morning
that his truck stayed. I assumed he must need something, so
I got up to see what was wrong. But when I stopped playing,
he left. After that I noticed he would stay almost every
delivery, twenty, sometimes thirty minutes. If I stopped
playing, he would leave."

"Did you talk to him?"

"No," Miss Wood said. "That would have been inappropriate. As it was, it was already somewhat inappropriate, since
we were alone together in the house."

"Wait a minute. You mean he used to come in and put the meat in your kitchen and sit there and listen to you play, and you never even spoke to him?"

"I never saw him, face to face."

"For how long?"

"Six years," Miss Wood said. "Then he died."

"How did you find out? Did he leave a letter for you?"

"No, no. One day his son-in-law came for the delivery. He told me that Louis had passed away. A heart attack."

"He didn't leave any—letters—or anything?" I couldn't believe it. It was the worst story I'd ever heard.

She shook her head, opening her little box, fishing for a star to paste next to her handmade one.

"But he did die of a broken heart," I said.

"Oh, Claire," Miss Wood said, almost laughing. Then she looked at me for a moment, trying, I guess, to take me seriously. "I suppose you could say that."

The oak lost its leaves all in a rush, and this was the weekend, a weekend of gusting, turbulent winds that sent them drifting across the field, into Genevieve's yard and beyond. With each rush of wind another batch would come loose and startle around us like a flock of birds. I watched them dramatically, waited for a lull to begin. Genevieve yanked down her hat, a green and white one with a big pompon her grandma had crocheted for her, her eyes tearing in the cold, patiently waiting. Ellen shivered, pushed her glasses up on her nose.

"After her mother died, he would come to deliver the meat," I said. "One day, he came in the back door and put the meat in the icebox, and he just stopped. He knew he should go, but he couldn't make himself leave until she finished playing the song she always played on Tuesday and Saturday mornings, when she saw his truck in the alley."

"What song?" Genevieve asked.

"'Pathetique.'"

Ellen gasped. "Just like she plays in—"

"Exactly. In lessons. You know how she always gets to that one part, and stops? One morning he was standing there, listening like he always did with his cap in his hand, and his heart just stopped like a watch. And he died, listening to that song."

"Just like that?" Ellen said, horrified.

I nodded. "So she always plays to that very moment when his heart stopped." I was borrowing heavily from a story my father told, about how Puccini died in the middle of writing *Turandot*. I looked at Ellen's face but there wasn't any sign of recognition—she was so gullible. "And when she came out she found him there, like he was still listening, just with his eyes closed."

"Didn't he fall?" Genevieve asked.

"He was sitting down," I said.

"You said he was standing up," Genevieve said. "With his hat—"

"He couldn't have stood that long," I said.

"Oh," Genevieve said, but she was eyeing me, her head cocked. Genevieve was the smartest kid in the ninth grade, maybe even the whole school. Not an easy kid to fool.

That evening my mother made a festive dinner, finishing with fruit salad and crème de menthe over ice cream, the menu standing in stark contrast to the atmosphere, the walls exposed lath with dusty plaster oozing from between the slats, the ceiling new blonde rafters and plywood with fresh lumberyard stamps, a dispirited light fixture hanging by a long gray wire, solemnly stapled in place. I was pondering Miss Wood, the thousand better endings I could come up with for her story. Miss Wood rushing into the kitchen, throwing her arms around Mr. Treski, a frantic movie kiss. Mrs. Treski dying, and Miss Wood marrying Mr. Treski, and taking him and all his children into her house, teaching his children piano.

Then I saw Miss Wood, hands hovering over the keys, her hair dark, let down over her shoulders, her eyes two black wells as she watched him walk away, week after week after week.

"I guess this is as good a time as any to tell you," my father said. "I got an offer from a company in Texas. Remember last month, when I went down there? It's a great company, right outside of Dallas. You girls won't believe the schools."

"We can't leave," I said. "The house isn't done."

"We'll pay to have it finished," he said, an answer, obviously, ready for everything.

"But you said we were staying here."

"I know, Claire, and I know how much you like it here. But this is an opportunity I can't afford to pass up. I found a house, a brand new place in a nice development. And wait till you see Dallas. You have to see the city at night. It's incredible." He looked back and forth between Ellen and me, gauging. "Dallas is booming," he finally said. "Toledo—Toledo's a ghost town."

John started asking him questions about cowboys and horses and hats, and my father jumped up to fetch some surprises he'd brought for us. My mother sat at the table, looking hopefully at Ellen and me. Ellen turned to me, her mouth opening, but I was already standing up and heading for the kitchen, out the back door.

There was no way to strike a dramatic retreat from the back of the house just then, as it was in the midst of an involved expansion, so I stepped carefully across the two-by-twelve my father had laid over the complicated pit below, future foundation for a back porch or a mud room of some sort. To the right stood our crazy old garage with its false front of stacked blocks, which made it look like a building from an old Western movie; a single light over the door cast a bright circle on our weedy driveway, the only unpaved one on the street. I walked behind the garage, climbed onto a palette of bricks, rested my back against the wall and contemplated our yard. Before the pink-streaked horizon the plants were crisp shadows, each stalk and leaf distinct before the fading light. Straight ahead a mound of asparagus swayed, chest-high; it had overwhelmed the twisted chicken wire fence and was advancing on the garage. I sat and watched the colors drain away, the plants lose their edges and lines. Somehow, I had missed the signs: my father waking up later and later in the mornings, falling asleep earlier each night with a *National Geographic* in his lap, a sweating scotch on the box next to his chair. Hurrying to work, coming home early. He'd stopped telling work stories a year ago or more, never talked about work at all, had stopped bringing home interesting glassware samples from the lab. The signs were all there, but I guess I had stopped looking.

It was dark when I went in to call Genevieve. "Meet me at the oak tree," I said, and even though it was cold and late and her hair was wet from her bath, and her mother was a stickler for that kind of thing, she didn't even ask what I wanted, she knew me that well.

That night, that swallow-you-whole sky was loaded with stars, and bent so low on every side it felt like it was pressing down on me as I scuffed through the empty lot, knocking loopy, cold-doped bees from the clover heads. Across the way, Genevieve's back door banged shut. I could just make out her figure cutting through the patches of light thrown down by her house, past each familiar bush, ducking under the split rail fence, a shadow person making her way diagonally across the field toward the oak.

At my last lesson, Miss Wood spent ten minutes writing elaborate notes for my next teacher, who didn't exist and never would. I didn't have the heart to stop her. She wasn't the first person ever to write to people who didn't exist, or to play for a ghost. We were not so different, Miss Wood and I.

I never went back, even though Genevieve invited me for years. But the longer I was away, the less I wanted to return and see how small the place must have grown, how sparse the stars, how perfectly ordinary the tract houses, how trim that mysterious house, the jungle of a yard. And even if I managed to pull off a feat—say I came at just the right time of year, and the neighbor's pear tree still stood, and I managed to find a late season pear in an early snow— would the voices of my friends come wandering down the dark road, calling my name as I bent down to claim it?

HERE

At seven every night two bats come down the street, circling one another as they fly between the trees. They travel twenty feet above the asphalt, hunting mosquitoes and moths. They look like rags operated by an inexperienced puppeteer. Sometimes in summer the children toss up stones to watch them dive. They don't seem to know stone from food.

A woman wearing a camouflage coat and black pants walks a black dog nightly. She comes out at the same time as the bats and follows the same route, head down, oblivious to traffic. The children call her suicide lady.

A man who lived on the end of the street committed suicide four years ago. He went on vacation and dove off a lighthouse. His wife was bewildered for a while, then moved. He used to rinse his driveway every morning and nudge acorns out of the cracks with the toes of his slippers.

She turns the tap. Steam swirls under her chin. She has the window open for a breeze but there is no breeze.

The children work at the table. They are learning to do bubble tests. If none of the given answers fits, instead of

NA for None of the Above, they are told to mark NH for Not Here. As if to say, there must be an answer somewhere but it's gone missing.

Moths bat at the screen, drawn to the light over the sink. When she turns off the water she can hear them hit, a splanging sound quiet as clothes dropping on carpet. They hold onto the screen with hooks fine as hair. They have mistaken a 60-watt bulb for the moon.

The moon is out, only it's 200,000 miles from here. Today it came out in midday, a bland blue picture hanging over the grocery store parking lot like a prop laid out in a hallway before a show.

The neighbor's porch light goes on. His wife died in the spring. They are from another era and still loved each other. Sometimes at night when she is out on her porch she hears him cry. His dogs are keeping him alive. They need feeding.

This afternoon she passed a farm where a sheep was cuddling up to a cinder block wall. Its chin was pressed tight against the block, eyes closed in sleep. She wishes she hadn't seen it, that black chin cocked against the block.

Her son has a question. She takes the paper from him and reads. A ring of suds radiates from her thumb and into the paper. It will dry crinkly but clean.

She dries her hands and moves to the table. She makes the lightest circles around their mistakes, erasable circles, and they make corrections. The answers are here after all. The moths hit the picture window, louder against the glass but still a sound one has to listen for. She read an article that said they're disappearing, fruitlessly courting billboards, soaring headlong into headlights, filling bug zapper trays. Fortune favors the bright.

One by one the children pack away their papers. One by one they return from the shower, hastily dried, and she tucks them in. Tell me what I did when I was little, her daughter says, her hair wetting the pillow, tell me about your childhood. What her daughter means to ask is, who were you, who am I?

You used to say hambubber, she tells her. Twice in first grade you rode the wrong bus home. Once you were jumping on the bed and knocked your teeth through your lip and had to get stitches. Finally her daughter smiles, satisfied. She remembers, she always says, even things that happened when she was too small to remember.

She reads stories to the baby. The old stories are brutal and she edits them, takes out the squirrel's heart in the box, the stones sewn into the belly of the wolf.

Her husband is asleep. The moths are at the windows, tracking the last light. Up close, they are unique. Some have shaggy legs and rust-colored manes like lions. Some have iridescent wings like the insides of shells. They are the colors of old pearls and bark and dried out cornstalks at sunset. They all have great black eyes and cannot help themselves; they see in every glimmer something shining, something beautiful, something they cannot live without.

She turns off the light and one by one the moths drop away, making the tiniest sound of all when they let go. Down in the back of the yard, milkweed leaves wave like white hands under the moon. Her husband stirs, reaches an arm across the bed. Where are you? he says, and she says, Here, I'm right here. If the children come in the middle of the night and say I'm scared she says, Here, and pulls them into bed.

How do you know, she wonders, when you've found what you were looking for? She has been a stranger on this road forever, hunting after things that shine; she still can't tell from the cast and fall of a thing whether it is food, whether it is stone.

The Reclamation Specialist

L ike most towns, Cope has had a succession of names, some more apt than others. It has had the good fortune of never being surnamed: Cope comes from "copse," although some, in this latter day, have wryly suggested "corpse." The Indians gave the area its first name, *Towamensing,* the wild place. None of these evoke Cope in its prime, when it was dubbed, however briefly and optimistically, the El Dorado of the great coal rush of 1829.

Cope is not approached from a distance so much as happened upon, a product of its twisted topography. To find it, one must wind through seemingly endless, identical green ridges that give way to further small, nearly vertical green ridges, till Mount Carbon bends away to the left and suddenly there's the white tower with its owl's-eye clock rising up from the trees, the fortress-like prison, a handful of bell towers and steeples. Farther down the mountain a line of buildings marks the course of Center Street through town, past Pomeroy's, the Necho Allen Hotel, the old dance hall, the granite First National Bank. At the foot of the mountain lie the low, long brick warehouses and sheds, the ugly networks of wires and poles, the railroad tracks and the Little Schuylkill, crossed by an aging cement bridge blackened unto a disarming beauty by grime and soot, being slowly invaded by honeysuckle and sumac.

Henry drives out of town, crosses the bridge and proceeds to the stoplight where Center Street dead-ends at Route 61. Straight ahead is a red-blue wall of rock so steep that people missing the light have, on occasion, run into it. A twisted, dented guardrail before it holds a large yellow reflective sign with arrows pointing left and right—any way but straight.

He goes right, turning his radio knob, squinting when he catches a snatch of conversation—gets a very tentative hold on NPR, as good a transmission as you can get up here, gently backs his hand off the button. He is driving north on an official visit to the mayor of Centralia, to make an offer he has made ten, fifteen times, maybe more over the past twenty years, an offer that has always been refused.

Henry is a reclamation specialist for the Pennsylvania Coal Commission, a job he has held since he graduated from college in 1981. The job, as it was pitched to him twenty years ago by a younger, trimmer version of Al Trucknick, the same boss who oversees him today, was to restore abandoned mining sites to their original conditions. It was a new position, part of an Appalachian recovery initiative pork-barreled into a military spending bill. Tobyhanna Army Base got a global communications contract; Cope got Henry Gray. That first year, Henry traveled the length of the coalfields taking water and soil samples, and drew up elaborate schemes for returning mining sites to their original conditions. Then the question arose of what "original" meant. Should he go back to the time of the settlers? Or before that, to the Native Americans?

(This eliminated a lot of "introduced" species the settlers brought with them, which some purists insisted on calling "aliens," as if they were from another planet). One day, about a year into his work, he looked up from the *Peterson's Guide to Eastern Forests*, where he had been reading up on the Ph preferences of lowbush huckleberry, and realized that he hadn't begun reclaiming anything.

Soil first. Soil, then flora, then fauna. The range and food requirements of the black bear, what it might take to entice the mountain lion back into these woods—all that would have to wait. He went back to the beginning, to the four-by-six-foot aerial map of the coal beds he'd had made for the wall opposite his desk, with pins of three different colors to mark the mine sites he meant to tackle: green for moderately damaged, blue, severe, red, urgent, 167 in all. There were a great number of red pins, a smattering of blue and a handful of green, a color scheme Henry had imagined slowly reversing over time. The immediate issue was the culm banks, sterile rock piles that the mines left behind, some—many—the size of small mountains.

For this, Henry adopted the methods of the coal operators who were already reclaiming culm banks for profit, capturing the smaller grades of coal—pea, rice and dust—that couldn't be captured or weren't worth bothering with back when the culm was dumped. In the beginning, in those first hopeful, naïve years, Henry had envisioned turning a profit, enough to pay for subsequent phases of the project, soil replacement, plantings, huckleberries and litters of baby mountain lions. Those hopes evaporated as he found that most of the large banks were coal-poor; the very rich banks had been cleaned out. Removing the excess stone would not pay for itself. Henry removed, every year, as much as the PCC's reclamation budget permitted.

He scaled back again, picking his top ten sites, the ten most urgent projects where he would focus his attention and budget. He planted ten tiny white numbered flags on his map. Trucknick applauded the idea—something to present at the quarterly board meetings. "Start small," Trucknick would say, encouraging him.

"You have to start somewhere," Henry agreed.

Immediate goals, small steps. That's what he's been missing with Centralia. Not the big picture, the whole complicated mess, Henry's come to realize this week, staring at the tiny white flag on his map, but the first step. All he has to do is change the mind of an eighty-five-year-old man. A Schuylkill County man, yes, a miner, no less, which means he's stubborn, but also proud. The more he thought about it, the simpler it seemed. Appeal to the man's pride.

He follows Route 61, winding in neverending S-curves between the tight little mountains, solid green like a bunched up, sculpted carpet, through thirty-foot roadcuts, past the Acme and the You Glo Girl nail and tanning salon. A mile later, the Pollack mink farm sign, a plain enough thing by day—a tall white sign featuring a black line drawing of a woman in a floor-length fur coat—but at night lit up in bright pink and blinking gold neon. The woman dates to the fifties or sixties, mod updo, hairband and bangs, trim skirt, one foot tilted up, hands on her hips. It only recently occurred to Henry to wonder why the mink farm advertises at all, let alone in this extravagant fashion. They sell their coats and stoles through stores up and down the east coast, certainly not from the farm. Every few years when PETA comes it just points the way for the protestors.

Sometimes the mink escape, and people living in the cottages down the road will report seeing them bounding through the grass.

Two miles outside of Lesser Shaft, where Henry grew up, he comes to his father's shop, a sight that always comforts him. His father died three years ago, but his mother and uncle and several cousins still work there. In a strange way, it's only Henry and his father and his little brother Michael that seem to have changed: his mother still does the books in the office in the back; old Mr. Katz still comes over to sit in the green vinyl chair across from her desk at noon every day to eat his sandwiches and wait for the mail to come so he can sort it. Uncle Hal is still stationed at his desk in the back office, golf clubs by the door, making deals on the phone before a glass case lined with football and baseball trophies from Henry's cousins, plus assorted vendor awards, a model car and, for some reason, a magic eight ball and a hula girl drink mixer. Uncle Hal has an entire desk drawer full of keys, and one of them—he doesn't know which—goes to the case.

The place is an old, windowless brick warehouse with parts shelves in the front and a garage in back, smelling of tires and oil, the floors padded black with grease, the air carrying remnants of music from the mechanics' radio back in the garage, the intermittent *zip zip* of the air wrenches. In the early days, back when Henry's father worked in the garage, they serviced big machines from the mines; today it's more fleet maintenance, truck and even auto repair. The school bus used to drop off Henry and Michael there every afternoon, holding up traffic on Route 61 to deposit them at the mouth of the parking lot. Henry turns in and parks next to the front door, takes a bag from the passenger seat and climbs the front steps. The old metal door is heavy as ever, the interior still dark and cavernous, but today the salesman's counter where he and Michael used to toss their book bags is empty except for two telephones and a couple of oversized binders. The salesmen were always good for change for the soda machine, which gave little scuffed bottles for fifteen cents, the kind you had to really yank to get out. The machine is still there, offering the same choices: Pepsi, orange, root beer, cream; only the price has changed. Henry plugs in three quarters, yanks out a relatively glossy bottle of cream soda, opens it on the bottle opener next to the change return, *galunk, clink-k-k.*

He proceeds down the hall, takes a swig of cold, frothy soda that sets his eyes swimming, opens a door with a frosted glass panel, the word OFFICE pasted on it in black and gold sticker letters. His mother is adding up bills, punching numbers into an adding machine that makes a pleasing crunch every time it prints a line. It was one of the mysteries of his early childhood, how it knew when to print red and when to print black. She'd always had interesting tools back there, an old check-writing machine that made pinprick numbers when you pulled down a crank arm, a cast iron notary seal that pressed raised letters into paper, a behemoth Royal typewriter that jumped on the typing el when you hit the "on" button and practically knocked you back in your seat when you hit "return." There was an old leather chair with rollers that you could spin on, and Michael would kick and spin, kick and spin while Henry clacked away at the keys, writing officious letters that always began, "To Whom It May Concern."

Return, return.

"Hey, Mom," Henry says, leaning down to give her a kiss. "I brought your hoagies," he says, laying a House of Pizza bag on her desk. She opens her purse and he waves her away, asks about her shoulder, which has been bothering her. She is still holding it hunched up, favoring it as she punches the adding machine. Hal and Katz overhear and quickly appear; Henry allows them to pay their odd dollars for their lunches, and enjoys a few minutes of small talk before he has to leave.

"I'm off to Centralia," he tells them.

"Not those kooks again," Hal says.

"Kooks—ha," says old Katz. "That last house went for more than a quarter million." Hal's eyebrows go up but his mouth is too full of meatball sub to expound on the matter. He's tucked his tie into the breast pocket of his shirt as he always does for lunch, held there by a Champion spark plug pocket protector. "Crazy like a fox, that's what they are," Katz says, squinting. He hears the mail truck and brightens up; Henry shakes hands, kisses his mother, confirms with her that he and Martha and the kids will pick her up for dinner Saturday at the Distelfink, and takes his leave.

Back down the long, bleak hallway crammed with free art: calendars and plaques from all kinds of companies, Goodyear, Firestone, Champion, Fram, plus local businesses, insurance agencies and hardware stores. He stops back at the soda machine, lets his bottle drop, shuddering, into the wooden case next to it and buys another one, waiting for each quarter to make its complicated descent into the hidden change box before feeding the next so it doesn't jam.

He drives for another forty-five minutes, eating his sub, going over strategy as he slowly winds his way north to Centralia, the town that has been on fire since 1962. In those days people were in the habit of burning trash, for reasons Henry can't really put together, on the culm banks. And while hard coal is notoriously difficult to ignite, once ignited it is equally difficult to extinguish. Back when he was a boy on long car trips north to visit relatives, they used to pass a mountain of culm that Henry's father said had been on fire since early in the century. His father would point out the yellow streaks in the snow where the sulfuric acid was condensing out. That fire burned until the 1970s, when they finally put it out by digging a pond and moving the culm with a dragline, dumping it shovelful by shovelful into the water, a process that itself took more than a year.

In Centralia the unthinkable had happened: the fire had gone underground, ignited a coal seam that probably runs from here to Jim Thorpe. The government has spent millions trying to put it out, and even more trying to convince the residents to move. But despite the fact that their town is now full of hot spots where plumes of sulfuric acid steam out of the ground, some people see no reason to leave. At night the hot spots glow like so many dying campfires as far as the eye can see; it is rumored that kids come out to roast weenies over the vents.

Since 1983, when the government appropriated a special fund for the purpose, it has been part of Henry's job to try to relocate the holdouts. Every year or so he comes up with an envelope bearing enticements, legal notices and threats for the remaining inhabitants, and every year they refuse through their representative, the mayor of Centralia, Charlie Tenpenny. Mayor Tenpenny now presides over fourteen residents in six houses—down from seventeen in seven, since one family just gave up, hence Henry's follow-up visit. They are always hoping for a domino effect.

He turns off the main road, follows a potholed, disintegrating lane over a slight rise and down into a broad clearing, grassy above, growing rocky and ashen, tarry and gray, in the middle. From the top of the hill you can see for several miles, green ridges bunched up one after another until they turn bluish and hazy in the distance. Henry directs his rusted Land Rover along the path of least resistance, the truck dipping and bouncing over the holes, slowly descending toward a line of trees halfway down the field that marks the beginning of town proper. Tufts of grass encircle large rings of charred ground; yellowing strands wave among the ashes. Smoke from several hot spots blows lazily uphill; the air is sharp with sulfur. To the left bordering the woods is a large plot of smoking ground where the fire is most active, blocked off by chain link fencing. Signs on the fence warn visitors to stay out, beware of poisonous gas, of the possibility of subsidence, when the ground opens up without warning and swallows things wholesale: big things, like cars, houses and people.

It's like riding horseback, big hip bumps below him as the Land Rover noses forward, down through the line of trees and into town. Maybe it's just the end of the ashes, but the grass looks emerald here, lit up by some trick of the light. Side roads lead off from the lane, forming an eerie, empty grid of sidewalks and streets that reminds Henry of the modern cemetery where his father is buried, a cemetery without headstones. He never liked the look of it, all those expectant pathways around what looks to be empty grass. His mother said it saves mowing and looks better. Henry prefers real graves, however inefficient.

Two blocks down, on the left side, is the property the people just left; a cement walk leads from the curb to a dark square of seeded earth, the footprint of the house. Across the street two of the remaining homes look on, both white wood with small porches, then an empty plot and a small one-story place sided in crumbling green asbestos shingles. Henry proceeds to Fourth Street, takes a right and stops before a lone house with blue aluminum siding. In the front yard is a metal swing hanging from a stand, a fat, matted white poodle napping on its flowered cushions. The poodle raises its head when Henry pulls up, then juts its chin and lowers it back between its paws.

Tenpenny greets Henry at the door, white hair slicked back, wearing a white t-shirt and green chino pants. He steps down onto the porch, reaching back to let the louvered screen door, which is cranked open to admit the breeze, ease closed. Down here the air blows up from the valley, and the sulfur smell is barely detectable.

It begins as it always does, Henry laying out the government's latest offers, Tenpenny listening politely, smiling up at him through thick bifocals. But this time, Henry pauses. The whine of a distant truck engine rises from the valley. Leaves rustle; the swing creaks.

"You know," Henry says, turning from the napping dog, the empty street, to look directly into Tenpenny's eyes, "being mayor is a position of considerable responsibility." Tenpenny nods carefully, his mouth drawn down, conceding nothing. "The others listen to you."

"I'm not about to tell anybody what to do," Tenpenny says.

"But that's just it—"

"They're all here by their own free choice."

"That's the point, Mr. Tenpenny. As mayor, you don't have to tell anybody what to do. They're following your example. You're their leader. You stay, they stay. You leave, they'll leave. Do you really want to be responsible if, God forbid, somebody gets hurt, or worse—"

"No one has ever been hurt by that fire," Tenpenny says.

"Yet," Henry says.

"This is the best town in the world, as far as I'm concerned."

"Town?" Henry says, exasperated. "What town?"

Tenpenny looks left, right, as if the answer to that were self-evident. "You know, Westons left because their kid went to Harrisburg. Not because of the fire. It isn't the fire that's killing us, it's the job market. You don't own a business, there's nothing to do up here, except work at the Acme. Of course, that doesn't matter to me, because I'm retired," Tenpenny says. "I'm going to die in this house. But it matters to our young people. That's what they should be looking into down in Harrisburg. You tell them I said so."

Henry nods, looking out at the mountains, almost wants to laugh. "The job market," he finally says.

"What is that work you do, again?" the mayor asks.

"Reclamation specialist."

"That's right," the mayor says with a little chuckle. Henry frowns at him, opens his mouth, shakes his head.

Once again, Henry fails to convince him. It's hard, after all, to bribe or threaten a miner. After surviving eighty-five years on the earth, forty-seven of them in the mines, the guy is correct in his surmise that a little sulfuric acid won't kill him. And if the ground decides to open up under his feet and swallow him whole after all those years it willingly spit him out day after day after day, well, so be it. Ashes to ashes.

He thanks Tenpenny for his time, pets his dog, which has finally hopped down from the swing and waddled over to investigate, and leaves him there, standing on the front porch with the envelopes in his hand, looking past Henry and his dusty Land Rover at the valley spread out before him. Henry opens his door, pauses, follows Tenpenny's gaze. He does, in fact, have a nice view.

Centralia shouldn't be on Henry's top ten list, not because it isn't dire—it's dire all right—but because it is beyond repair, beyond reclaiming. He put it on the list more as a matter of form than anything.

Before leaving he does some surveying, measures temperatures with a probe in holes they've drilled for the purpose. He measures outside the fenced area and marks the readings on a grid for his files. He gets a reading over 600 degrees on the southern end—not promising. Within the fenced areas he has seen temperatures of 1,000 degrees. His quarterly report will include a revised map, projections, a recommendation to extend the fence fifteen feet south. An account of his meeting with the mayor.

When he is finished he drives through the smoking field, back over the crest of the hill to the shade of the road, and he cranks the windows all the way open and starts breathing deeply again, gratefully inhaling the cool, fresh air flowing out of the woods on either side. The late afternoon sun spindles over his windshield; he sees fiddlehead ferns curling up from the ground, skunk cabbage in full leaf, here and there a dogwood. The coal region, stripped, sifted through, used up, acid-washed, devastated, nonetheless has a determined beauty, an undeniable, rugged kind of charm. The radio has gone to static. Henry turns it down. He hears, instead, Tenpenny. Hears himself.

You stay, they stay.

There's nothing to do up here.

Henry had never intended to stay. He'd just come home the summer after college, answered an ad and got the job. The following summer, while he was contemplating graduate school, he met Martha, also home for the summer after her graduation. The following June, as if his life were on some seasonal cycle like the wheeling disk on a grandfather clock, they married. He can't imagine his children—Rachel is in high school, Sam and Bobby in middle school—staying here.

From space you can see the hard coal region for what it is, Pangaea's wrinkled fender, the aftermath of a colossal collision when Gondwana (Africa lumped together with India, Eurasia and Antarctica) smashed into North America more than 250 million years ago, just before the dinosaurs came on the scene. The wrinkles even follow the curve of the western coast of Africa, so you can almost imagine it in fast-forward, the crash and the rebound that is still happening today. It was the heat and pressure of that collision that compressed the regular coal (the soft, bituminous coal that fueled Pittsburgh steel, which most in the hard coal region regard as best suited for backyard barbecues, or making artists' sketches) into the east end's singular prize: anthracite, up to 98 percent pure carbon. Two percent more and you'd have a diamond. When he'd bought Martha's engagement ring, that's how Henry had seen it, pure carbon. Sunlight swallowed up by the earth and spit back out as sunlight again.

The first time he'd seen the maps of the coal beds, back in middle school, Henry had stared. It was hard to imagine, living here where coal was and still is everything, that it all lay in these tiny strips of land some hundred and forty miles wide. He wasn't sure what was more shocking, that anthracite was so rare, or that they, the coal region, were so small.

After Rachel was born, he and Martha bought an old house on Norwegian Street, at the end of "mansion row," a tall, white painted-brick place with black shutters and a massive porch, a place that would cost a fortune if it weren't in Cope. It's one of those old town homes that look magically lit up from the inside in winter, removed from ordinary time, snow drifted to the sills, overgrown evergreens leaning in at the windows as if they, too, were charmed by the view. It makes Henry happy, walking up evenings, seeing his family inside that grand old place, having family over at Thanksgiving and Christmas. It's almost too late to move; Rachel is in band, the kids have friends on the block and at school. To his children, Cope is home. And their father is a fixer of mountains, or as Martha likes to tease him, a mover of mountains, a joke he once enjoyed that now brings a twinge of pain. He tries not to think about how little of those gravel mountains he has actually moved over the past twenty years, about the mammoth pair of banks out near Bethlehem, sterile, lunar and terrible, number one on Henry's top ten list, that are only about fifteen percent smaller than they were when he came in. In twenty years, he's never made it past soil. Never made it *to* soil, in fact—he's still struggling to make a dent in rock. Now in his forties, Henry is just beginning to square with something he probably recognized years before, but didn't want to admit to himself: that is the work of another lifetime. Of another's lifetime.

Early in his career Henry wrote a slogan that was such a hit it became the commission's tagline: "The PCC: Bringing together the needs of people and of the earth." They print it on the PCC's annual calendar under sparkling pictures of the Schuylkill River in spring, or of tumbling cataracts and groves of rhododendron in the Lehigh River Valley. It's printed on the brochures Henry hands out during his rounds of coal talks at the local schools and universities, about how valuable it is, how the industry is working to restore the land. About all the coal that is still up here, eight billion tons of it, how they'll surely be back for it when the market is right.

The truth is, Henry isn't sure he could live anywhere else. Whenever he drives south to Harrisburg, when he crosses over the broad Blue Mountain and sees the farmland stretching out beyond Route 78, so featureless and empty and flat it makes a gas station feel like an event, he feels a little sick at heart. He doesn't consider that newcomers who somehow, by plan or accident or for adventure, find their way up into the hills of the coal region might feel the same sick sense of loss over their fertile fields, their pumpkin farms and farmers' markets, their open view of the sun. It's always with a sense of relief that he climbs over the ridge of the Blue Mountain and drops, rapidly accelerating, back into the valley beyond.

He rounds a bend and there's the Pollack Mink Farm sign, lit up now, the woman traced in hot pink, the sign in gold. It is dusk and the neon shines against the still-light sky with that eerie, jarring, plaintive glow of light out of step. Around the edge the gold chaser lights march in a blinking stream up, up and around the glowing woman, down the other side, back up to flow into a giant arrow.

This way, it says, over and over again, *this way*.

He pulls into the Acme, stationed at the back of a weedy parking lot exactly twice the size it requires. He needs softener salt. While he's at it, he'll get a couple of cases of soda, heavy things that bother Martha's back. His cart has a renegade front wheel; he commandeers it by brute force through the aisles. On his way to checkout he sees a sale on Tastykake snack pies, three for a dollar, picks up twelve. The fixtures could go directly out of service and into an antique barn: here is a metal rack featuring the Sunbeam Bread girl, biting into a well-buttered slice of white bread, here another display features the Coppertone Baby's white bottom, her swimsuit tugged down by a tiny terrier. The store is deserted. An old man in a red apron bags Henry's pies, takes stickers from the cashier and puts one on each bag of salt, each case of soda.

He wrestles the cart, which has grown even more unruly under weight of the salt, back through the entrance, rattling across the pebbly parking lot. He nears his truck and is feeling for his keys when he glimpses something moving at the far end of the lot. The light is uncertain, so he has to look hard, but then he sees them, leaping through the weeds, two slender, graceful shadows so foreign in shape and gait that for a moment he cannot place them; they seem to belong to another world.

ANATOMY OF STONE

The sun pressed like a heavy hand on her head, coaxing out the smell of her shampoo, soap, a damp shower smell. Ninety-three million miles away, yet even with her back turned she could feel when a cloud passed over it—the hand lifted, a sharp chill replaced it until the cloud cleared, then it was back, cupping her head. A distant lawnmower engaged, making listening to the guide even more difficult, but he was finished anyway, motioning them to follow. He walked toward a cluster of buildings, rather thoughtlessly themed, Molly thought—covered wagon, mining chute, Batty the plywood mascot, a log cabin gift shop complete with resident limping collie. The bat was kind of cute, and the dog was a given, but the pioneer business was a bit of a stretch. According to the brochure, the cave preceded the settlers by a good 40,000 years.

The crowd waded deliberately through the tilted grass, so overgrown that it snagged their sneakers and tickled their ankles. Molly believed she could smell the grass cut by the mower, or it could be this grass, which they were lightly juicing underfoot. The guide stopped at the top of a flight of cement steps leading to the cave—122 of them, according to the tour brochure, a fact the guide affirmed before starting down. Molly let the other kids count them, focusing on the steps themselves, which were, as all significant steps seem to be, oddly spaced and the wrong height to boot, inspiring an awkward, chicken-necking descent. At the bottom, instead of a cave, they found a stream nearly out of its banks, something that was not in the brochure, a roiling, muddy creek speeding past only twenty, thirty feet away, almost on level with the clearing where they stood. After school, where everything had warning labels and finger guards and safety treads, it seemed almost inconsiderate. The kids stared at the sticks and leaves and shreds of plastic caught in the current, bobbing on the surface, rolling under, and it was so muddy and ugly that even Cory and his friends, the freshmen rowdies, stayed back from it.

"We've had a lot of rain; the creek's a bit full," the guide said. "Please stay back along the bank here. We're heading this way." Only then did Molly turn left and see the unlikely black hole in the wooded bank facing the water. The guide was already striding toward it, and the kids followed, tripping over hard ruts in the dried mud, climbing the narrowing trail into the trees by twos and then alone. The sun retreated, drawn up high into the leaves overhead; a current of cool air flowed over their legs and arms, replacing the heavy, eggy smell of creek water and warm skin with a mineral smell, the smell of cement after a rain. The smell grew stronger as they entered the mouth of the cave, blinking and untying their jackets from their waists.

Molly followed the crowd, still half-blind from daylight, down a short flight of stone steps to stand in the center of a cavern that looked less like a natural wonder than a highway underpass—cramped, dirty, littered with graffiti and abandoned fire rings. Next to the stairs, a Plexiglas box marked "TIPS" cradled a single, folded five-dollar bill, a feeder, no doubt. She pulled on her jacket and tried not to think about the weight of all that stone and dirt pressing down overhead. Logically, it couldn't stand forever. How could anyone measure exactly what the roof could hold, or when it would fall in? What was holding it up at all? If she were to ask, she knew they would say, it's been here for thousands of years, the odds of its caving in this afternoon are minuscule. But some day must be that day.

The guide, who stopped at the doorway to wave them through, cut through the crowd to reclaim his place in front and asked them all to line up, tracing a line on the floor with his flashlight. It took a few minutes, but he finally got them into a line two-deep that nearly spanned the cavern. Molly managed a spot in the second row. "This line," he said, sweeping the beam across their shoes, "is the farthest point light can reach in this cave. The Susquehannock, who were the first people we know of to use the cave, used it for meetings, for shelter, to store food, to hide from enemies, that sort of thing. But in all the years that they used it— maybe hundreds of years, for all we know, maybe even thousands—they never stepped beyond the spot where you're standing, because the Susquehannock would not walk beyond where the sun touches. To do so, they believed, would bring on a cursed life."

"Ooh," one of Cory's friends murmured, and a couple of kids laughed.

"Today, of course, people are not so superstitious. So, if you're ready, step right in," he said with a little smile, and then he walked off into the cave.

As soon as he turned his back, the kids in the back pushed the kids in the front over the line. Cory stumbled forward and clutched his neck and said, "I'm cursed," and his friends tumbled in behind, grasping each other's coats and yelping for help. Freshmen. Molly shook her head, rolled her eyes at the girls next to her as they fell in with the group.

The cave changed abruptly. The floor, which was gray and chalky back by the entrance, darkened; water streaked the walls. The ceiling sloped sharply and the floor with it, and after a short dip and a climb the whole place opened up into what the guide called the cathedral, a great hall with columns of rock rising forty, maybe fifty feet. Other tour groups were gathered there, pointing up at the formations, passing through openings that led off from the central chamber. Their voices were small but persistent, echoing emptily from the rock like cicada song. Something cold hit Molly's cheek, a large drop of water that splattered and left little shining drops on the lashes over her right eye. She blinked and wiped them away with her coat sleeve and another fat droplet hit her bangs. She looked up, ducking just as someone said something about bats, an alarm that traveled quickly through the crowd. But overhead there was nothing but the rock ceiling, dotted with tiny stalactites. The guide reassured them that it was very rare to see bats here, that even if they did see a bat, it wouldn't harm anyone, that the water dripping on them was clean enough to drink. Beneath the voices she could hear the water, too, a pattering and shushing, something wet underlying the ceaseless echo of the place.

The guide used his flashlight to point out shapes in the columns: a spider's web, a pouncing T-Rex, Rapunzel's tower, a pair of rearing elephants. It did not take much imagination to see what he saw and more. There was something grotesque about the rocks, maybe something to do with the yellow lighting, which came from spotlights down on the floor. No, it was the rocks, too. They were bulging and knuckled and sinewy and slick, nothing like what rock was supposed to look like, what it looked like above ground. It was flowstone, the guide explained, stone being worked by water. Flowstone was the stuff hanging in tiny, dripping strings from the ceiling, piling up underneath in odd, blubbery masses. Little blobs of it were scattered over the floor, all leaning in the same direction, listing uniformly downhill like a herd of petrified slugs.

"My group, over here," the guide said, gathering them before a set of crude cement steps with a skewed metal handrail. "We'll have more time to explore the cathedral at the end," he said. "For now, stay close together, please. It is possible to get lost in here, and I can tell you from personal experience, it isn't fun." He started up the stairs, then turned and added, "And, please, try not to step on the flowstone. It is growing."

This wasn't easy to do. The stuff was dripping over the edge of the railing, oozing over the lips of the steps, and sure enough Molly saw one of Cory's friends step on a little pile of it and turn his foot, crushing it the way someone puts out a cigarette. A girl behind them (a freshman, no doubt) chastised him, and Molly overheard Cory tell her, "You do realize this is a cement floor? They poured it in the fifties when they opened the place. Well, sure, look at it." Which Molly did, and saw it was of course poured. It was smooth and gray underneath all the blobs of gunk.

For the first fourteen years of Molly's life, Cory had been her best friend. He lived at the end of her block, and they used to climb on Molly's swingset, ride their bikes, play PIG on Cory's perfectly flat driveway. They saw one another through several basketball seasons; Cory made travel team. But then Molly went to high school, and suddenly the fact that Cory was a boy and two years younger began to matter. Despite his new dufus act, Cory was smarter than anyone she knew. She doubted that his new friends could appreciate that.

The guide stopped to show them a little side cavern where a fur trader once lived for several years, sleeping high on a stone ledge that looked like a perfect little stage set in the rock, right down to the twin spotlights shining up from the floor. One night his campfire asphyxiated him, the guide said, turning his beam on the ceiling to show where it was still black from the smoke. He was discovered thirty years later, lying on the ledge like Rip Van Winkle. "Trader John is still here, buried ninety feet overhead that way," the guide said, pointing with his flashlight, and Molly remembered they were under a grassy field, a big empty field with a split rail fence and a flag flapping on a pole like a sheet on a line. She found that hard to believe.

"It's one of the cave's many mysteries," the guide said, taking on a somber, funereal air, "why the smoke suddenly turned on Trader John that one night, after he'd spent so many nights sleeping here, in this very spot." He ran his light over the ledge again, frowning up at it as if it might reveal some new clue. "Some have speculated that ice may have formed in one of the vents, sealing off the flow of air. Others believe the Susquehannock had it right, that Trader John ventured in too far, and brought the curse of the cave on himself." The guide looked gravely at the empty ledge for a moment before turning to the crowd and saying, "So. Who wants to go farther in?"

He ducked quickly into a passageway. The group followed, spread out and quieted by the path, which narrowed to three, four feet wide in places. It was drier and darker here than in the cathedral, and the walls looked more like proper rocks, but white veins like lightning spread across them, and crystals of unusual colors jutted from the stone—red, amber, yellow, green. They passed small, anemonal growths the guide claimed were alive, white, glassy little fungi that sprouted from the rock. When they passed close to one, the guide said, "Be careful," and Molly wondered what he meant, whether he was trying to protect the crowd from the fungus or the fungus from the crowd. She thought of her uncle, who used to warn her away from the coral down in Florida, how he said it would slice her foot open if she stepped on it, and if a little piece of the rock broke off, it would grow inside her. She used to picture it laying hold of her, growing into her bones, making them spurry and sharp and lethal from the inside out. A couple of years ago she'd found out that wasn't true. She read in one of her science textbooks that coral could not grow inside the human body.

But fungus could. There was a man, Mr. Spellman, who stood up once at church and said they'd found a large mass in his lungs, and the doctors said it looked like cancer, and the man prayed, and when they did surgery they found not his own human cells gone haywire but a fungus bigger than an outstretched hand, a big mushroom blooming in his chest, which they simply cut up into pieces and extracted from him.

Which led Molly to believe just about anything can happen.

A chain of purple amethyst stretched from floor to ceiling in one little chamber, a ready-made museum piece; in another, the wall opened up at waist level to reveal a pond that stretched back into the rocks. Underwater lights made the water glimmer like a swimming pool, throwing quivering reflections around the sand-colored walls. She lingered by the shining pool, watching the bands of light tremble and flex on the stone, on the trail of pennies and dimes lining the bottom, which seemed magnified by the clear water. The coins scattered and disappeared as the water receded into the rock, and Molly wondered how far that water might go, how far back into the earth, for miles, maybe? And how deep? And were these caves everywhere, just underneath the lawns and the houses and the streets and fields where she walked every day, giant upside down cathedrals where crystals grew like houseplants and stone went creeping across the floor?

She was in the back of the group then and could barely see what the guide obviously considered the height of the tour: the bridal chamber. From where she stood Molly could see a big cavern, brightly lit, with what looked like table sugar everywhere, mounds of sugar and rock candy, sugar in a great waterfall frozen overhead, big jagged chunks of clear crystals pointing up from the floor. Before the opening, she saw Cory's silhouette, leaning in, mouth slightly open. Molly smiled—the geek in him was coming out. He was frowning down at a big column of crystal, absorbed in it, his new class-clown friends forgotten. Just then, as still happened frequently enough to constitute a running pain, she missed him. They'd never fought, exactly. They were just arguing over something small, and Cory threw the basketball at the ground and said, "You've changed," like that was some sort of crime.

"You're supposed to change," she'd said, in the same accusing tone. Which was true, she reminded herself, watching Cory on the far side of the cave, his profile— familiar, yet unfamiliar—against the rocks. Maybe.

"This is as far as we're allowed to go," the guide said, although the caves went on for miles into the earth, he assured them. Then he said, "Now I will give you a taste of the true darkness of the cave, the darkness in which all of this was made, in which some believe it was meant to stay." Molly found it odd, looking at the almost absurd mountain of crystals behind him, that such shiny things would grow precisely where they could not shine.

"I want to warn you that this is going to be completely dark," the guide said. He was a good showman, into the job, not just reciting his script. "If you are uncomfortable with that, please follow the lighted trail back to the main hall." He traced the path with his light. Voices rose; people snickered, but no one took him up on it. He shrugged. "Okay," he said. He went over to a metal box, flipped a switch, and then turned off his flashlight. For a moment it really was dark, dark like a presence against the eyes, and Molly felt her heart beating in the hollow at her neck, her eyes blinking to no effect—they made a tiny creaking sound, she realized, a muscle sound—but then a rim of light edged in, a remnant of light spilling in from the path behind them, and Molly could distinguish the outline of the boy standing in front of her. He moved and his jacket rustled. Someone whispered, and someone else shushed her; a shoe scuffed. Molly wondered what it would be like to be here in the dead dark, alone. Would it be peaceful, comforting, even, like sleeping? Or would it be terrible? Would she hear the rush of blood through her body, the water moving through the stone? Would it be like being submerged in the tub when the house was quiet, the sound of her heart loud in her ears? Would she know up from down? The guide switched on the lights again and everyone straightened, as if they couldn't feel how to stand up properly without the light.

They were free to explore, the guide said, but he gave them instructions first. "Stay on the path at all times, please don't throw anything in the water, and whatever you do, *don't* break off a piece of stalagmite to take home. Don't even *touch* the rocks, particularly where they're wet," he said. "A single fingerprint takes three hundred years to wash away. Beneath that spot, the stone dies."

Molly watched the guide for a moment, looking for a sign that he was having fun with them, but he seemed serious. Still, she was not sure she believed that.

She wandered ahead of the group, walked back out to the main hall, stared up at the trolls and sheep and hammers poised overhead. The columns grew slow as time, a quarter of an inch every hundred years, some slower yet, so a single inch represented four hundred, eight hundred years; the big towers were inconceivably old. Against them she was—what? A sliver, a layer of molecules, maybe. She stood next to a smaller one, only nine or ten feet, a young column, still narrow in the center, and tried to calculate the years.

She heard a yell, and saw Cory trip, stepping into some rocks in a brightly lit enclave about thirty yards away. "You killed it!" his friend said, making a great show of pointing and laughing; Cory gave him a half-hearted shove back. Molly could tell he was annoyed. Then he glanced up and saw her. She turned back to the column, tried to count off inches, tried to concentrate. The columns were beautiful and hideous at the same time; they had spikes like teeth and tusks, knobby ridges like spines, stuff that looked like baleen and brains, everything but rock, and all of it veined and taut and wrinkled and seeping minerals, seeping iron and calcium and salt. She wanted to leave. Water hit her shoulder, the back of her head. She shook and stepped aside. She couldn't get used to it, this hysterical weeping, these bloated bones, this upside-down lighting. Another big drop hit her hard on the forehead and she stepped aside again, looking up, and maybe she did lose her balance a little, or maybe she liked the idea of leaving an imprint here, the mark of her hand for a few hundred years, but she was thinking, this is not a troll, that is not a sheep, this is not alive, when her hand came down.

DEPARTURE

A human brain is hardwired to assemble faces. It will piece them together compulsively out of whatever is at hand—a crumpled bit of paper, moon craters, rock formations. A woman in Florida saw the face of Jesus Christ in a burnt potato chip. Another managed to sell a grilled cheese sandwich for $28,000 because people saw in it a shadow-portrait of the Virgin Mary.

Sometimes I'm afraid I will forget your face.

Babies come into the world knowing what a face is. Presented with a simple black and white picture of a face, a baby will startle and babble to it, will strain to touch it. They're born looking for it, the watchful eyes, the mouth signaling approval, opening to speak.

Maybe it was just that—you seemed, for a while, to approve.

Whatever template it is a baby brings out of the womb—however that's done—it's inside the baby before the baby's vision develops enough to see a face. Maybe it's a statistical average of ten thousand years of human faces, maybe something derived from blinking in the dark, the thumb in the mouth, finger curled over the nose. Over time, that original template, which we can only guess at, merges with another, specific face: one's own. Children learn to draw themselves first, projecting their own features onto flowers and lions and mom and dad. Even as adults, most people, when pressed to draw someone, will draw a compromise between the subject's face and their own. Whenever they doubt their eyes, the hand splits the difference.

No, it was this: I could see you. I saw what you could do. I saw the artist. I saw the man. It was my own power, my only power—to see.

When seeking mates, people respond to those faces that most resemble their own in proportion, particularly in the set of the eyes, not because they mean to, but because it lines up with the template. Some biologists attribute this to an evolutionary drive to preserve one's genes. It's just as likely, though, that the brain clings reflexively to the self as a way of denying that there's a world entirely without it in the first place, a world self-sufficient and whole from which it might be erased without consequence.

And in you, not what I am, but the very thing, everything, that I am not. Your ego. Your certainty. Your fearless eye, almost a cruelty. Your expert hand, creating, ruining, telling the truth.

To make a picture, an artist must learn to see beyond the template. Amateur artists continue to paint themselves into every face they attempt; an accomplished artist trains the eye and hand to seek deviation. This is critical because the human face is most beautiful in all the places where it breaks the rules. To get at the beauty of a single face—to get at the truth—requires a kind of distortion. A well-drawn portrait, or that most fearsome of pictures, the caricature, goes directly to those places where the face is most distinctive and exaggerates, or at least elaborates, them.

If I had the hand I would draw your true lines, all the beautiful departures.

A brain confronted with the back side of a hollow mask becomes disoriented. Because it is hollow, the mask throws shadows on the wrong sides of its features, the sides facing the light. Unable to reconcile this, the brain turns the image inside out to create a whole, round face. To see it as solid, the brain merely accepts that the shading on the face is backward.

I would start with your eyes, but I can't even say what color they are. I could only look from the side, checking the sun, a hand deflecting. Eye color, the simplest of facts. Without study, you know, there is no way to it. Everything must be drawn from life, you said. *We like best that which is most true.*

If the mask is mounted on a stand and rotated, the brain is put in a further predicament. The shadows, which were backward to begin with, are suddenly also moving in the wrong direction. The brain resolves this by concluding that the face must be moving the opposite way. The result is a disturbing illusion: the real, solid mask rotates in one direction, and then the projected face rotates in the opposite direction, only to be swallowed up by the solid mask again. Every brain will do this, and will do the calculations automatically. The mind would rather buy a lie, turn the world inside out, than lose the face.

A slippery thing, the truth—just as I was reaching out to tip up the chin, smooth aside the hair, struggling to see— your face was already turning, turned away.

THE SPEED OF SOUND

A new moon and a clear, cold Michigan night, the sky dead black and loaded with stars, so clear you could see the tendrils in the Milky Way dust—things were aligning, and Arthur Reel was prepared. He called the two neighbors across the road, who were kind enough to turn off their automatic lights whenever Arthur said he would be skywatching. Three a.m. found him perched in his rooftop observatory, sitting in his padded folding chair next to a telescope that was almost as big around as a basketball, waiting. He was there to watch Leo rise, Leo with its telltale sickle, the backward question mark, although to Arthur it would always be Hook's hook—his son James had renamed it, along with most of the constellations. It had always puzzled James, made him indignant, in fact, how none of the constellations looked anything like the things they were named after, and who could argue? Even with the aid of an illustrated chart, it was hard to make out a lion in Leo, and as for Aquarius, forget it.

Hook was a far better name, Arthur thought.

He'd come up almost grudgingly, girding himself for disappointment because the Leonids were notorious, peaking for just one hour, almost too far north to catch, and yet so spectacular that few amateur skywatchers could resist the temptation to at least show up, just in case. It had already been a good year: he'd seen a nice Capricornid shower in July. Then in September in *Sky & Telescope,* some French astronomer had predicted "a chance for a brief Leonid outburst in 2006." A chance for people like Arthur, who missed the historic showers of 2001, when the meteors rained down at the incredible rate of 480 per hour. And as the date approached and the conditions fell in line one after another, he'd calmly made his plans to set his alarm and come up.

He'd just unscrewed the top of his Thermos when he saw something blaze straight out of Leo, a bright thing slipping almost too fast to follow across the sky. It left a trail, a pale streak with just the slightest arc, and Arthur stared, counting off seconds without meaning to—he'd heard the Leonids could hang in the air for minutes, they're so bright—when he felt hot coffee on his leg. He jerked his leg and tried to right the Thermos, but the more he turned it, the more it poured, and he realized the floor was rotating, tipping up from the right until it was vertical, then beyond, overturned.

He dropped the Thermos and tried to stand, but pitched over instantly, getting bungled up in the chair. He turned over on his knees, made for the open trap in the floor, which was also rising, rotating sickly counterclockwise like everything else. Later he remembered clinging to the stair rail, then a hard fall. After that, rolling. He would recall later it felt exactly like rolling a plane.

For four years before college Arthur had served as an Air Force pilot. In his last assignment, he flew F-89 Scorpion fighter jets out of Thule Air Force Base in Greenland, 700 miles north of the Arctic Circle. The base ran strategic air defense along the Canadian border, the DEW line, distant early warning, guarding against Russian planes. Any plane entering radar range of Thule was greeted by an F-89, lofted within three minutes of the first blip on the radar. If it was deemed hostile, which never happened on Arthur's watch, the orders were to come in at a ninety-degree angle and salvo the entire payload of 104 rockets at the target, because it was understood that if the F-89 missed the target on the first shot, she would never get a second. The newer planes were lighter, faster, more advanced; the F-89 was heavy, designed for a single purpose, no great maneuverer, not a plane you'd want in a dogfight. Unlike most planes, which lift off the runway when they reach a certain speed, the F-89 could make five hundred miles per hour on the ground and never bump a wheel. "You got to nudge her up," the instructor at Moody, a kid from Georgia, had told him. "Otherwise, Lieutenant, what you got here is basically a very big, very heavy, very fast automobile."

It was, in fact, an old bird even back then, but the F-89 was a fun plane to fly, Arthur would tell his kids, and perfectly good for the mission, as the odds of engaging anything were very low—particularly since any engagement was likely to set off World War III. The idea was deterrence, a visible presence, and for that the F-89 was well suited.

Usually after making contact and calling in the numbers, Arthur and his radop would fly over the mountains to burn off the fuel—it was that or dump it, since it wasn't safe to land fully loaded—and they would turn on the music, military radio KOLD out of Thule, and do Aileron rolls and Immelmans, sometimes buzz the tankers on the lonely road to the bay.

The Air Force limited duty at Thule to one year, for a reason. Thule tended to make people alcoholics, whether they were genetically predisposed or not. Six months of daylight, followed by six months of night, unshakable cold, and nothing to do off duty besides sit in the club and drink. At Thule you couldn't trust your own eyes; day was no longer day, night, no longer night. Even the compasses were wrong there, off by a full ninety degrees because the base was just east of magnetic north.

Arthur served an extra tour there, eighteen months in all. When he remembered Thule, what he remembered first was not the cold or the hardship, but the sky. In Thule the sky and the water were both indigo, a shade of blue Arthur believed only existed in that place, the water just a shade darker, set off by white glaciers. You could always find Thule from the small lopsided one just east of the base in Baffin Bay. The sky was cloudless, and even in the heart of the dark season it never quite went black, but just turned darker blue, like ink. Arthur thought it must have been the snow, reflecting light from somewhere, maybe even the dim light from the stars.

Arthur awoke to a bright, empty room full of harsh sunlight. It poured in a solid block through a large window to his right, lighting up the sheets on his bed and the dingy white curtain hung alongside it. The sound of a television on low volume came from the other side of the curtain, some game show, people applauding, and he felt the uncomfortable sense of being intimate with a stranger, made worse when the stranger coughed and cleared his throat. Arthur noticed the coarseness of the sheets, the smell of his blue gown, something between petroleum and soap. A bad, metallic taste in his mouth. A curve of flesh under his right eye that wasn't usually there, pushing up from his cheek, moving back and forth as he turned his head to try to look at it.

He remembered falling and realized he'd survived. Some kind of attack.

He turned his head toward the window and felt painful stiffness all the way down his neck. The aqua curtains on either side of the window were pulled back, giving Arthur a view, made hazy by streaks of dried-up rain, of a neighboring brick wall. Susannah had been here. She would have opened the curtains, frowned at the dirt and the view, reconsidering, then left them open for the light. Susannah had to have sunlight. This was determined light, mid-morning, he guessed. The sun lit up each drop of fluid that gathered and fell from the IV bag next to his bed, making it look precious.

He heard a creak, a whoosh; the curtain swayed. His wife appeared, purse tucked under her arm, a magazine in her hand. They looked at each other, surprised.

"How do you feel?" she asked, coming to his side, leaning down to give him an awkward kiss, just making contact with his hairline.

"What happened?"

"It wasn't a stroke," Susannah said. "They're running tests but they don't think it was a stroke. The doctor said it could be a mini-heart attack."

"A what?"

"Sometimes you can have a slight blockage, I don't know. Let me call the nurse and tell them you're awake again." She pulled a pager from the side of his bed and pushed a button, giving Arthur the impression she'd been here for a while.

"Again?" he said. "What time is it?"

"Three-thirty."

Arthur sat forward instinctively—he'd lost an entire day. He needed something for his head, that was all. Some strong pill to kill the terrible ache radiating from behind his eyes, pushing on his teeth, his skull. "I'm fine," he said. "I need ibuprofen."

"You fell on concrete. Arthur, nobody said you could get up," Susannah said, taking his forearm anyway as he moved his legs over the side of the bed.

"I have to go to the bathroom," he said. He felt her watching him and was glad for the IV pole, which he used to steady himself. For a moment when his feet hit the clammy floor, it seemed like the room was shifting, and he was afraid it was happening again. He breathed deeply, pushing the pole around the end of the bed just as the nurse came in. Arthur made an awkward introduction of sorts and nodded toward the bathroom.

When he was back in bed, lightly sweating, nauseated from the effort, he began to sort out what day it was. Friday, six days from Thanksgiving. "Did you hear anything from James?" he asked, while the nurse pumped up his blood pressure cuff.

Susannah shook her head, eyes on the nurse. The light flashed off her glasses, shone through her hair, fine as cobwebbing. It was a little flat. He could tell she hadn't showered, but she had carefully applied her makeup, here in the room, probably, using the makeup she always carried in her purse. Trying to keep things together.

The doctor came in shortly, a bit young and chipper for Arthur's taste, though Susannah seemed to trust him. He was thinking vertigo, he said, a little mix-up of the inner ear that makes the body temporarily lose its ability to tell up from down. Still, he would need more tests tomorrow, and Arthur had a low-grade fever. The upshot was, Arthur was stuck there for the night. Just for observation, the doctor added on his way out, as if that made it any better.

Susannah would have to drive the twenty-five minutes home, and another twenty-five back with his cholesterol medicine and the various supplies he needed to get through the night. Her entire evening would be eaten up in the car while he sat here being observed. Arthur apologized, urged her to take her time, eat dinner, call Carrie and Matthew and tell them he was fine. As she walked out, he thought to ask her to bring the *Scientific American* from his nightstand.

He watched the space she'd left, watched the curtain sway and settle, fighting down the frustration that welled up as soon as she left the room. A rush of tears, insistent as tiny fingers, prodded hidden spaces behind his eyes, deep in his head, spaces already tender and swollen. He blinked hard, took a slow, deliberate breath. Why now, of all times? He knew it was a childish impulse, knew that at his age, he should be grateful it wasn't something worse. But James was due in any day now, Wednesday night at the latest, for his first Thanksgiving home in six years, and that was where Arthur needed to be. Home.

James was nearing the end of his final tour as a Night Stalker, a special operations transport unit of the 160th Army Airborne Division out of Fort Campbell. His battalion flew specially configured MH-47E Chinooks equipped with long-range fuel tanks, multimode radar and infrared sensors—black, unmarked helicopters that could fly all but 150 miles per hour just a few feet off the ground or over the trees, in any conditions—dropping off and retrieving special ops troops on missions in Afghanistan and Iraq. He'd had mountain training, had done HALO jumps, had learned Arabic. Arthur and Susannah knew little more about their son's service than that. Because of the sensitivity of his work, he disappeared for six or eight months at a time. Arthur never knew specifically where he was, what he was doing, or when he would resurface. When he came home—long, scraggly hair, beard grown out—he never told them what he'd done. Painful as it was to go without word for these long stretches, Arthur pointed out to Susannah that James was probably safer in his unit than he would have been in most others. It was definitely safer than the infantry. Every month that went by without news meant almost certainly that James was still accounted for. The Army knew where he was from mission to mission. They had results to track.

During his time in the 160th, James had been home five times. Two were in the first year. The last time was eighteen months ago. So when he'd called in September to say he had leave for Thanksgiving, possibly through Christmas, Arthur and Susannah were elated in the measured way they'd learned over the years, knowing that there were good odds, at least even odds, that those plans might change. His leave might be withdrawn at the last minute, as it had before, maybe even suspended right through April, when his tour ended.

But then he'd called again two weeks ago to give them the number of a flight from New York to Detroit, arriving Wednesday. He would probably make it in earlier, but that flight would be his fallback, he said. Susannah had missed that call; she'd gone to the grocery store, which was probably why James said what he did. After he read off his flight information, he'd hesitated, then said, "Dad—just between us—if anything ever happens to me, if they say afterward I was spying, or doing anything other than working for the Army, don't believe it. Okay? Everything I'm doing is under orders of the Army."

"Of course," Arthur had said.

"Everything's fine, I just—if anything happens, they're going to tell you whatever suits the unit and the Army. They're under no obligation to tell the truth, not even to you. You understand that, right, Dad?"

"Of course," Arthur had said again, of course he knew that. That's what they do. Still, it had unsettled him. Since that afternoon, he'd run many possible scenarios through his head, trying to imagine the set of circumstances that would lead James to tell him that at all, let alone then, when he was due home in two weeks. Stuck in bed, with nothing to do but watch the light creep across the wall, he ran through them again. Most likely, it was something James had been saving up to tell him, something they talked about in special ops, and he had just decided to say it then because Susannah wasn't on the phone.

Arthur had never minded James's secrecy. In fact, he found it almost comforting. He sensed that the details would prove more worrisome than the wondering, for one thing. And it was part of the Night Stalkers' pledge, *I guard my unit's mission with secrecy, for my only true ally is the night and the element of surprise.* And Arthur knew that following orders, following his training, gave James the best chance of making it home.

The next morning, after a bizarre test involving blurry glasses and a swivel chair that struck Arthur as disturbingly low-tech, his diagnosis was confirmed. A spell of vertigo, something Arthur could cure with a pill whenever he felt an attack coming on. Probably had something to do with the frostbite he'd suffered in his left ear at Thule. "I'd avoid roller coasters," the doctor said, giving Arthur's arm a little shake. Arthur accepted this gesture gamely—good news is good news, after all—and agreed to come back for some tests early the next week.

That afternoon, Arthur went back out to his observatory. He climbed the spiral stairs deliberately, his hand a little tighter than usual on the rail. Susannah hated those stairs, so steep and winding, and they struck Arthur as twisted now, narrower than before, the gaps between treads wider.

He'd purchased the observatory, a nine-foot, fully wired dome unit, as a kit over the Internet three years ago, after he got his new Celestron CPC 800. He designed the platform for it himself, and built it into his garage roof, just under the peak on the north side. The dome was generous by home observatory standards, but still quite small, just big enough for two chairs, a running ledge for the equipment, and his scope, which was mounted to a cinder block column that ran down to the garage floor. The stable mount allowed him to get deep space images, the kinds he saw in magazines. The dome had retractable roof segments that afforded a full 360-degree view. With all the vanes open, on a clear night, the sky seemed so vast and so close overhead it was disorienting, as if you could fall up.

The Celestron was an automated scope. It relied on global positioning systems to lock in targets, the same systems Arthur had worked on in his job with Syncrotek, which designed the GPS technology for General Motors in Detroit. The Celestron used global positioning only to locate itself. From there, it located everything in the heavens with astonishing precision, deducing the location of each space object in relation to that single orienting point. The CPC 800 was a technological leap; older scopes, without that absolute starting position, could only point to the neighborhood of an object. Even they were an advance over pushing the telescope around by hand.

He flipped a switch and a gray light filled the room, just enough to work by but not enough to feel lit, the sort of dull, inadequate light found inside a ship or a plane. He never liked the feel of the observatory by day, even with the dome opened wide. The daytime sky looked small in it, daffy even, and the room felt smaller somehow, too. It was a room made for a purpose, made for night.

The last time James was home, Arthur had brought him up after dinner. It was James's first time in the observatory, and Arthur wanted to show him what the Celestron could do. It turned out to be a poor night for skywatching, cloudy and a waxing moon, and they weren't up there half an hour when Arthur turned around to say something to James and saw that he'd fallen asleep sitting up, the side of his head tilted against the metal base of the scope. Arthur put off waking him. He powered down the scope, straightened his papers, and then just sat, watching James sleep, watching the clouds make their slow progress across the opening overhead.

I pledge to maintain my body, mind and equipment in a constant state of readiness, for I am a member of the fastest deployable Task Force in the world—ready to move at a moment's notice, anytime, anywhere, arriving on target plus or minus thirty seconds. The pledge James took. Arthur wondered, not for the first time, whether he'd charmed James into the service with his stories about the scrambles, his tall tales of the planes. The F-22 Raptor: the pilot's dream to fly. The SR-71 Blackbird ramjet that broke Mach 3.2, so fast that the cockpit smelled like a self-cleaning oven in flight. So fast that it couldn't even be fueled up on the ground, because it leaked fuel all over the place until it reached speed, when it grew a full two inches and everything sealed. So fast that on its trial run, the tires exploded in their bays.

How many times—two, three?—he'd taken the family up to Wurtsmith in the years before it closed, eating picnic lunches in the parking lot, then standing by the fence, watching the F-16s come out of the hangars, shimmering in the fumes and the heat, the crews running through their checklists, the twenty-foot flames as the afterburners kicked in, the roar and the plane ascending, always rolling off to one side. The coordination, the precision timing. Arthur thought that the whole family enjoyed the trips, but James was always the last to leave the fence. And the last one awake on Arthur's skywatching vigils, the one who never tired of deciphering the charts, back when they used the Meade and they had to find everything by hand.

Arthur pulled up his files from the night of his attack. He stopped at a frame and, in spite of the tender stiffness in his face, smiled.

Sunday afternoon, Carrie came with her family. Arthur assured them that he felt better than he looked, which was good because Arthur looked pretty bad. The right side of his face was bruised from his eye down to his jaw. His eye was swollen; two spots on his cheekbone were bright red. Carrie's older daughter, Amanda, was afraid at first—she was only eight and very sensitive, Arthur thought. He let her touch his cheek, assured her it didn't hurt. And then said, "But look what I got for that shiner," and brought them all back to his study.

He showed them his photo, a bright fireball with a sky-long tail tracing all the way back to Leo. "The Hook," Carrie said, touching it with her finger.

"Hook's hook," Arthur said, smiling, and then showed it to Amanda. "See it? And that," he said proudly, "is one of the fastest meteors in the world. That meteor was traveling 44 miles per *second*," he added. Before long he'd opened his display case, and was passing around his collection of mail-order meteorites, specks of dirt in little plastic boxes with somber labels, *Shergotty (AEUC) Achondrite, Shergottite SNC Signature Meteorite, Fell: September 10, 1935; Location: Gaya, India.*

"Does anybody verify these?" Carrie's husband asked, frowning down at one of Arthur's specks. "What do they go by, the composition?"

"That's part of it," Arthur said. "Although often after a big shower they'll find scattered debris. Sometimes you can actually see them fall."

"It looks like dirt," Amanda said.

"That's a shooting star, honey," Carrie said.

"No, you're right, Amanda, that's just what it is," Arthur said. "Shooting stars aren't stars at all. They're just ordinary rocks. In fact, these are big ones, these made it to the ground—most shooting stars are no bigger than a grain of sand. And yet you can see them from hundreds of miles away. Know why? Because they're going so fast they blast the air into plasma and it phosphoresces. They're going so fast they make light."

Amanda looked puzzled, handed it back to him.

"How do you like that?" Arthur said, gazing at the bit of rock in his box. "A grain of sand."

Monday morning, Arthur returned to the hospital for scans and more blood work. It was after lunch before he sat down with his doctor. This time, no tousling, no roller coaster jokes. They'd found spots in his scans, several in the region of his left ear. He showed Arthur an image of his head, with little fuzzy areas like mothballs. "Here," he said, "and here."

"So, what do we do?" Arthur said, catching himself in the medical "we" he'd adopted from the doctor, shaking his head.

"I've asked an oncologist, Dr. Bodner, to join us. She should be here in a few minutes." Arthur blinked at him— first a kid, now a woman—not that he didn't think a woman could do the job, but just the intimacy of it. He'd rather take it from a guy his own age, preferably one who was falling apart at roughly the same rate as Arthur. But the kid was assuring him she was the best, and Arthur was trying to pay attention. "Surgery may not be possible, given the locations," the doctor said. "She'll discuss your options."

"Options," Arthur said, choices to make.

"Either way, you'll want to begin chemotherapy right away. I might expect as early as tomorrow. Unfortunately, Mr. Reel, this is a fast-moving cancer." Arthur watched him fiddle with the flap of his coat pocket, pull out a pen. "I'll let Dr. Bodner explain," the kid said uneasily, checking his watch.

"What happens if I do nothing?" Arthur asked.

There's one antidote to fear, and it's training. You do the right thing over and over in practice, Arthur liked to tell his grandkids. Then, when the time comes and you're in an emergency, you do the right thing without thinking.

By Wednesday afternoon, they'd had no word again from James, which was unusual even for him. Arthur and Susannah busied themselves through dinner—it was his last window, in New York, to make a call before boarding the commercial plane, his fallback flight. When the call didn't come, Arthur had a giddy sense that James might ring the doorbell instead, might appear with his bags on the porch, wave goodbye to some stranger in a pickup truck. James's plans had changed many times before, but he'd always called at some point to cancel or confirm.

"He probably lost his leave," Arthur told Susannah, who was chopping onions and mushrooms for the stuffing. "He probably didn't get a chance to tell us."

At seven-thirty, Arthur said he would go meet the plane James had reserved, even though he thought it unlikely James would be on it. Susannah agreed, reluctantly, to stay home. "He'll probably call while I'm on the road," Arthur told her. "Just call me and I'll turn around."

Sitting in a little plastic chair, bolted in a line before a large bank of windows, Arthur reconsidered their last conversation, what James said. He'd probably lost someone in his unit; maybe someone was killed and he'd heard rumors afterward about differing accounts of the death, the official report given to the family. Probably one of his buddies talked to a wife, something like that. Stuff like that got around. Arthur had read stories of body laundering in special ops, bodies doctored to match stories told to the families.

Once Moscow Molly had said in a broadcast, "To the boys at Thule—the lights at the end of your runway are out." And the guys in the tower looked out and they were. It was understood up there who the enemy was, where the boundaries were, what it meant if they were crossed. And it wasn't just the troops, back then, who were in a state of constant readiness—it was the country. People built bomb shelters, stored food, something the kids laughed about today. They couldn't fathom it, didn't realize there was a time when the cold war was very close to becoming a hot one.

James's war was different.

Often when Arthur told people, usually in answer to a direct question, where James was or what he did, they'd do a little check, then recover with something like, "Oh, yes, that's terrible, isn't it?" And Arthur would realize they forgot we were at war.

But there's no comparing then and now, Arthur often said. Things were slipping; he couldn't necessarily relate to them the peculiar smell of brown Fels Nap soap, the way Lynn Fontaine said "I love you" and it sounded like she meant it, the hot chocolate in little hockey pucks. *Lucky Green has gone to war.* The queer satisfaction of field dressing a cigarette, pressing the paper into the earth, invisible.

For a while when he was a boy, Arthur had believed that all the sound on earth traveled forever into space, the result of misunderstanding something his father told him about radio transmissions. Some years later he'd realized his error, the difference between electromagnetic waves and sound, which is a pure compression wave, a clumsy thing, stuff bumping into the stuff next to it, which bumps into the stuff next to it. Not like light, part particle, part wave, which could travel two paths at once, could travel through space for a hundred million years to bounce off a patch of snow. Much as Arthur enjoyed reading about the new physics—god particles and quantum uncertainty and multiple universes— he had to admit that most of it had very little to do with life on the planet, which tumbled along, day into day, and traveled only one path, and petered out.

A woman around Carrie's age walked toward him, took in his face, then looked hastily past him, trying to be polite. She sat in a row of chairs across from his, looking nonchalantly everywhere but at Arthur. He felt the need to explain his appearance, to tell her it's okay, I just fell.

In the black space beyond the windows, practically obscured by the harsh airport lights, tiny blinking lights floated silently in the sky. Every so often a pair of them would line up with the runway, seeming to hover beyond it, then finally descend, the shadow of the plane spreading between them. There was a chance James was on his plane. He'd have a story to tell when he got off it, some crazy story about getting dropped on the tarmac, jumping out of an unmarked black Chinook. Something to explain where he was, why there wasn't time to call.

Trajectories

Our spring picnics came early. One morning after months in the house I would open the front door and smell dirt, and by noon we would be at a picnic table by the pond, the two of you shivering in your spring coats, wind tugging at the Styrofoam cups until we could get the cocoa in them. The dirt on the island was powdery and was attracted to the cups by static—if they got away, which they sometimes did, they were unusable.

You were babies then. I miss you already, even while you are asleep in my bed with the white morning light poured over you like protection. Love is an arrow.

A large bird came across the water, so big it never even flapped its wings. It cruised swiftly around the pond, moving without moving, silently pacing its shadow over the water. It was out of scale, out of place in this dinky municipal park with its lawn sprinkler fountain and weeping willows and wedding photo gazebos, the pond choked with bloated, overgrown carp.

After my mother died, I drove her wheelchair out of the hospital. As I backed it up to the van, I caught people inside staring out at me. Did they pity me? I wanted to explain that they were mistaken. This is not mine. My father chained the chair to the lift and pushed the lever. Rising from the curb, my back to the van, I felt what she must have felt: helpless. On display.

Separate.

What brought it here from the endless waterways it must belong to, why it would choose to settle on such an unpromising patch of dirt in the middle of town, was beyond reasoning out. We were still staring—everyone stared—when it drew up ten feet from our table, wings folding back, legs dangling like strings, hanging on the air for a moment with a couple of quick flaps before easing down to a spot on shore. The fat geese hissed and scattered, grudgingly clearing a place for it. And only then did you turn and say, "What is it?"

I empty the upstairs closet. I find clothing dating back to her college days, outfits that I recognize from old photos still matched and hung with paper between the folds. We go through stacks of papers and pictures and cards, envelopes and shoe boxes and folders. "She kept the books until that final week," my father says, handing me the checkbook. "It was always dead accurate." The entries on the last several pages are nearly illegible, traced and retraced until they dented the paper.

On the ground it was a completely different bird. Suddenly slight, a tiny oval of body poised between slender legs and neck, beak fine as the point of a pencil. It stood on the bank, turning its head this way and that, eyeing the water for fish, so unlikely in the midst of the petty geese, which were still jutting their necks and honking their objections. They left a wide circle on the dirt around it, a perimeter. "I think it's a heron," I said. "It must be a long way from home."

Sometimes our picnics were so early the grass was still cupping snow in the low spots. Back then it took me more than two hours to move us all from house to car to picnic table. It was a production. We had the time, so that was okay.

In this picture she is seated in a webbed lawn chair, smiling. She only smiled halfway to hide her overbite. She combed her hair forward over her ears because she thought they were too big. This posed a challenge, since her hair was very fine. According to the Bible, our hair is our glory. It is to be worn long and flowing, a feminine crown. For both of us, with fuzz for hair that would never grow past our necks, this reads as just another accusation. *Mene mene tekel.*

My father takes the picture from me. "God," he says, "she was beautiful."

Everything came to you so much earlier than I expected. One night when I tucked you in I felt tears on your face. "What's the matter?" I asked, imagining a missed party invitation, something mean or careless said at school, but instead you said, "I don't want to die." You were only eight or nine years old. "Oh, honey," I said, running quickly through the potential responses, choosing carefully, "when you die you'll go right to Heaven, and I'll already be there waiting for you. You won't be alone for a second. I promise."

"But I don't want to go to Heaven," you said. "I want to stay flesh."

In this photo, she is standing in the dark, holding a balloon, pregnant with my older sister. It's an experiment in strobe photography, and her faith in my father, who got her to stand for the picture, and in his lab partner, who fired the gun, must have been absolute. At the moment of the flash, a bullet is passing through the balloon, which is half missing but still fully inflated. From the perspective of the bullet, it must be carving through a slower space. From the perspective of the balloon, and the air, and my mother, it outruns time.

On the fourth day of her stay, my father and I had finally seen what was happening. We were sitting in the hospital coffee shop. We'd both reached the conclusion, and merely had to say it. "I think," he said, "I don't think she's coming home." "I don't think so, either," I said, or "I think so, too." "I think we're talking palliative care," he said, a word he was clearly testing out. And having the word let us move forward, proceed through what came next. Upstairs, the oncologist came from her room and asked us to join him in the consultation room, where he tried very diplomatically to break the news to us. We waited politely for him to understand.

"I know," my father said. Then he said, "I think we're talking *palliative care* at this point."

Everyone who sleeps is an infant.

This is my favorite picture of her, even though I'm not in it. She is bent over, fixing the hood of my big sister's coat. She has a scarf wrapped around her head, and long white socks with loafers and a long tan woolen coat. I love the picture the most because in it she seems so in her time. She was happy then, with everything before her.

One night I came to tuck you in and found that you were already asleep. When I kissed you, you said, "I can't, I'm busy working." I had to know what job you, at twelve, would have dreamt for yourself. "Working at what?" I asked, smiling, and you rolled over and murmured, "At not dying."

The brochure from hospice was titled, "Killing Me With Chicken Soup." The hospice woman explained that my mother was involved in a complicated process, and the IVs were just getting in her way. The dying, she explained, don't need what we need. Not even water, she said.

It presided for several minutes before some boys came with sticks and chased it away. It lifted unsteadily, wobbled a moment before stabilizing on the air. Suddenly it was substantial again, neck tucked in, those great black wings. The geese quickly closed the circle, satisfied.

In sleep we can step across time easy as Jesus walking over the face of the water. What are you staring at? he asked his friends. Haven't you heard a word I've said?

The hospice woman bent over her and patted my mother's head and said, "It's okay to go now, Marilyn. Your husband and your daughters will be all right. You can let go now." I opened my mouth to object. My father's mouth opened, too. I realized then we'd been keeping a sort of pact, one we hadn't discussed or even thought through until that moment, not to let her know she was dying. Ever alert to the potential benefit of a good, timely lie, we had only said, "Rest. Rest so you can get better, rest so you can come home."

A strobe is the simplest of mechanisms. Combined with an open camera shutter in a dark room, triggered by sound waves from a gunshot, it allows a person to capture a god's-eye view of the world. The resulting photograph reveals something impossible, something unrecognizable slipped in between the jumbled envelopes of time.

Impossible things happen every day, our pastor used to say.

Breathing was the last thing to go. I am still not sure, but it seemed to me she had died overnight, was already dead when I arrived in the morning. Her eyes stayed open all day, but they saw nothing. Her mouth was stiff, frozen open. Yet she breathed until evening. And then, as the hospice person was standing before us, still talking, I saw the breaths spread apart. One took a full minute. The next, longer yet, and that was the last. After the hospice woman left, my father tried to close her mouth. It was stuck, bloody, impassable. Her temples were hollow, her hips and stomach like a girl's, her body ninety pounds. I closed her eyes with a tissue because I was afraid to touch her.

The funeral director, for reasons of her own, I imagine, as we hadn't asked, gave us the official cause of death: cancer, along with a secondary cause: dehydration. I wanted to recall the hospice woman. It was all a bit pointless by then. My father was testing out another word: cremains. This one seemed to help him along, as he used it several times over the next few weeks. Then the funeral director said, "Her mouth? Was that the cancer, I assume?" As if even she, boatwoman over the River Styx, had never seen anything like it. As if my mother might have been more graceful about it.

That spring a baby bird fell on our driveway. It had a nearly bald head, hollow temples, beak open, legs slighter than twigs, a tiny ribcage clenched like a hopeful fist and underneath something tender, a little yellow ball of organs. It felt like an oyster in my hand.

In this photo, she is majorette. Her hair is combed forward, but she has the mercy of the tall hat and plume. She holds the baton proudly, one leg cocked up in her majorette pose. She is a member of the band.

I recognize her sometimes by my car. She is asleep. She steps across time easy as that and casts her awkward shadow by me all the way home. She hangs on the air, moving without moving, pacing over the face of time. Oh ye of little faith, she says. Find me some water.

I saw them one morning on a sunny hillside so green it looked like the start of a movie. Black crows, wings tucked back like great thinkers, striding through the grass. Her mourners. Her companions.

Our kind.

We lie in the slow, safe darkness and I listen to you fall asleep one after the other. It's all right, I tell you. It's okay.

I am the man behind the curtain, worriedly pulling my levers, keeping up the show. The secrets I keep I cannot keep forever: impossible things happen every day. The bird in the air is heavier than the one on the ground. It moves without moving.

We are miles from home.

THE UNIVERSAL PHYSICS
OF ESCAPE

Examining convergence to understand complex brain functions is especially exciting when phylogenetically remote animals like cephalopods and vertebrates exhibit similar forms of complex behaviors . . .

Apart from the evolutionary significance of the octopus, several practical reasons make it highly suitable as a subject for research on the neural bases of complex behavior. Firstly, it takes only a few days for an octopus to adapt to captivity. This adaptation, or acclimatization, can easily be perceived by humans, as it involves a clear transition from a frightened, hiding octopus to a pet-like animal that behaves in a friendly way and attends to any event occurring in its aquarium area . . .

A second reason for the octopus's suitability for research on the neural basis for complex behavior is that the animal shows highly stereotypic predatory behavior, which is easy to activate (e.g., by offering a crab tied to a string) and to quantify. Furthermore, due to the octopus's natural 'curiosity,'[1] this pattern of behavior can be initiated by various artificial targets, thus creating conditions ideal for visual discrimination experiments.

> Third, octopuses are resilient to invasive surgery
> and recover rapidly following lesions in their central
> nervous system under deep anesthesia.
>
> —"The Octopus: A Model for a Comparative
> Analysis of the Evolution of Learning and
> Memory Mechanisms," Binyamin Hochner,
> Tal Shomrat and Graziano Fiorito.[2]

She bends forward, pushing back a cumbersome, invasive purse (which frequently distresses her by banging into people in crowds, ruining her otherwise perfect unobtrusiveness, but which she nonetheless carries because it is a gift, and expensive, and holds an entire magazine without the need to fold it) and sees in the tank before her something foreign but unmistakable: an eye. It pops out from a piece of PVC pipe affixed to the bottom of the aquarium and floats there, bobbing on the end of a slender stalk, swaying in the water. It seems, if she is reading it correctly, to be squinting at her.

"Guys," she says without moving. "Come here." Another eye springs from the tube and nods in the water, looking directly at her.

"Mom, they have an eel back here," her daughter says, coming down the aisle.

She drops the heavy purse from her shoulder and puts her hand up to the glass as Lily moves in beside her. Several slender white feelers slip out of the hole, tap the lip of the pipe and latch onto it; two more unfurl into the water and reach up toward them. Bubbles shoot from the back corner of the tank and swirl around like space dust in the water. The eyes and, disturbingly, the head of the octopus sway with the currents, never still.

A loud clank comes from the next display, which makes the octopus flinch. A worker is changing a piece of equipment. Pumps whir and buzz; the whole place is working loudly like a ship or a large factory. Water is splashed on the floor, pooling in the low spots under the rows of tables, puddles permanent enough to be sprouting bits of vegetation and scum. The man responsible for the noise is bent over the next tank, examining some mechanism; the back of his t-shirt features a large orange wave with "Instant Ocean: Just Add Water" printed over it in bright purple letters. He looks like a seaman—rough beard, green knit cap, big yellow Wellies, a product of his environment, certainly, if a bit out of place, given that the ocean is three hours east of here.

Lily jogs down the aisle to fetch her older sister, eager to show something new to her for a change. The octopus is half out of the tube now, several arms reaching out into the water, the rest firmly suctioned to the pipe. It is unmistakable: the thing is eyeing her. When the girls appear the octopus draws back and flushes a muddy olive color.

"Cool," Samantha says.

"I didn't know they changed colors, mom," Lily says.

"Me neither," Claire says, moving her hand down. Just then it lets go of the pipe and flows, (it doesn't so much swim as *billow*), eyes first, its body hanging from the two stalks, a sack of—what, she doesn't even know—brain? bouncing behind, and attaches to the glass near her hand. She moves it left and the octopus follows. Its suckers press against the glass like little hungry mouths, pressing flat, then letting go. Lily puts her hand up by the top of the tank and the octopus climbs toward it. Several tiny legs roll and unfurl in the churning water at the surface.

"Look at its legs," Lily says.

"I think they're tentacles," Samantha says.

"Actually, they're arms," the Instant Ocean man says from the next tank. "Squid have tentacles. Octopuses just have arms. No cephalopods have legs."

"Oh," Lily murmurs politely, and Claire offers a barely audible thanks, but he has already turned back to his task. Samantha gives him a quick appraisal, a half-smile, no doubt thinking something along the lines of "Gorton Fisherman." At fourteen, she has a well-developed sense of irony, a mixed blessing, her mother thinks, one of many inherited directly from her, but there it is. In the past year, she has grown more than two inches. She is already taller than her mother.

Lily moves her hand, leading the octopus along the wall. In the old days, their game was going from tank to tank to find any creatures that were hiding out in their little plastic pipes. Back then, Lily had to stand on tiptoe to see in, or be held up to the glass. She used to say "pee-boo" instead of "peek-a-boo." Now she stands eye to eye with the octopus, which is patting the glass methodically wherever it spies a finger.

"Weird," Samantha says.

"Oh, it's so cute," Lily says. "Can we get it, Mom?"

"I'm sure they're complicated to keep," Claire says. "They're saltwater—creatures (she'd almost said fish), so you'd have to have all the right chemicals, and the right temperature—they're very sensitive. Anyway, remember the goldfish fiasco."

"Huh?"

"The algae? Mr. Snail? Maybe you were too young."

"Aw, it's lonely," Lily says. "Why'd they put it in there all alone?"

Lily looks at her, expecting an answer, and for a moment, Claire considers asking the Instant Ocean man. But his back is turned and he's bagging some fish for a customer. The girls watch the octopus for another minute before Samantha says, "Come see the eels, Mom."

"Yeah, come on, Mom," Lily says, tugging on her hand.

"In a minute," she says, and bends back down to the tank. She puts her hand up again, about a foot from the octopus. It turns immediately, creeps along the tank toward her and aligns itself with her hand. She moves her hand up and it follows, eyes bobbing wildly in the turbulence, the sac of its head denting and deforming. Several arms breach the water's surface, rolling in the bubbles.

The tank is double-walled, with a row of tiny holes following the waterline of the interior tank, and the octopus feels through them to the wall beyond, its arms slipping through and stretching out like tiny earthworms. It tries one arm after the other, patting frantically at the glass beneath her finger. She is troubled by it, and hesitant to leave. But she hears the girls coming back now, calling for her. There are eels to see, and crickets to buy for the girls' anoles.

It swaps arms again, the whole time watching her. Arms. Not tentacles, not legs, he said, just arms. For holding on.

She works three mornings a week at the Please Touch museum in Lancaster, trying to set herself up for some kind of career now that Lily is almost through elementary school. She was hired because of her astronomy background, but many mornings she is confined to restocking the plastic groceries in the faux grocery store, or sorting the magnetic gears and wooden arms into their proper bins in the Dream Machine corner.

Looking back, she isn't sure why she had majored in astronomy. At the time, she'd assumed it was more practical than painting, her other passion then. It has struck her since that painting, here in Lancaster, is probably the more practical after all. She knows a woman who has built an entire business out of painting mailboxes and birdhouses—landscape elements, she calls them—while Claire has found it difficult to translate her studies into any kind of vocation. Getting this spot, where she occasionally gets to deliver the

Wonders of the Night Sky show to school groups, had been a triumph.

She finds Lee Morris, the museum's director, in the Creature Corner tending one of the box turtles, a female that started nesting and was moved to her own tank. Lee has a doctorate in paleozoology, but like everyone in the museum he works in a catchall capacity, tending live animals and rocks and whatever else he takes an interest in, or no one else happens to. "We have a tour at nine," he tells her, taking off his gloves and replacing the lid on the tank. "Sixth graders from Stedmyer. I thought we'd do the planetarium at 9:30, before they get too rowdy."

"Thanks for that," Claire says, smiling. Once they'd saved the show for 11 as a grand finale. One of the kids shot a gear from the Dream Machine into Regulus. It took them two days and a full set of scaffolding to remove it.

She holds her hand over a heat lamp attached to a long cage by the door, home to Gomer, the eastern rattlesnake. "What do you know about octopus?" she asks, turning her hand in the heat.

"Oh, octopus are awesome," Lee says, kneeling on the floor and rooting through a cupboard under the displays. "Why?"

"They have one at the Fish Place."

"Really?" he says, adding to a growing pile of junk on the floor. "Is it for sale? They don't generally sell them."

"Why not?"

"They don't live very long. They're terrible pets."

The rattlesnake stirs in its artificial log and slides out onto the sand. As if the name weren't bad enough, he is molting, and has a flake of skin sticking up from his nose. Lee says he's the world's only neurotic rattler.

"Still, they're really cool," Lee says, finally finding what he's looking for. "I'll have to stop in and see it." He starts repacking items in the cupboards in no particular order, ensuring that the next search for goods will be equally random and difficult. "What did you think of Dawkins? Did you start it?"

"He's amazing," Claire says.

"Did you get to the bar code part?"

"I don't think so."

"You're going to love that," Lee says. "It's right up your alley."

The kids arrive, and Claire takes a familiar position in crowd control. She guides a third of the children through their first station before all of the groups gather in the planetarium. She turns the lights down as soon as the last student finds a seat and launches immediately into the show. Sixth grade is actually a good year. Kids are still interested in science and game enough to want to answer questions. Besides, the planetarium has a naturally calming, distracting effect. Few can resist the cool darkness, the illusion of sky overhead, and apart from the occasional kid who falls asleep, it is usually easy to keep their attention. She follows the script. Brightest star in the night sky? How many of you say the North Star? Please, be *serious* . . . She explains the history and use of the constellations, how they helped hunters and farmers and sailors memorize the night sky to track their own steps. She points out that most of the constellations are not groups of stars in space, aren't anywhere near each other, in fact, but are chance alignments based on our perspective. She goes through the old tales, reliable Orion and his battle with Scorpio, the Great Bear and his band of weary hunters, vain Cassiopeia enthroned forever on her head, another mean trick by the old gods.

She hits a switch and the heavens disappear, replaced by a looming plaster ceiling. Even the children stare for a moment, trying to reorient.

Her group finishes by building rocket ships and other machines out of blocks and gears and connectors in the Dream Machine. Here, anything goes. The only limit, Claire says, still on script, is your imagination.

Like Pluto, the big extinctions have seen a bit of a demotion lately. Some scientists now believe that even the P/T, the "Great Dying," which extinguished around 70 percent of land-dwelling species and 96 percent of sea creatures, may have been not so much a massive catastrophe as a series of painful adjustments.

Life persists, and errors just become new code.

Octopus is old, even by the Earth's standards, and it has therefore seen its share of disasters. Its roots reach back into a common nautilus ancestor some 500 million years ago. It's hard to believe, but at the time, nautilus was a top predator, a terror of the sea, with some growing as big as millstones. About 400 million years ago, for reasons that are still unclear, the cephalopods gave up their shells and branched off from nautilus. Some scientists believe that both species survived the Great Dying by taking to deep water and, in the case of the nautilus, seriously scaling down its ambitions. When the ocean acidified and oxygen levels plummeted, shelled animals and those near the surface were hardest hit. Octopus and nautilus, buried in the depths of the waters, survived on the fringe.

Today, octopus have moved back into niches throughout the oceans, from shallow waters all the way down to the abyssopelagic zone. One species of octopus has been captured at depths of 7,000 feet. While the species has diversified widely, its basic body plan bears the mark of its time in deep water. Their blood is blue, based on hemocyanin, which carries oxygen effectively in the cold, low-oxygen conditions found in deep water. Hemocyanin is only one fourth as efficient as hemoglobin, however, so while humans can oxygenate all of our systems and extremities with one heart, octopus requires three.

Creatures without shells or bones, of course, leave a poor fossil record, so octopus's deep history, like a lot of things about the octopus, is speculated rather than known. But even the briefest look at its body plan makes one thing clear: by any standard, the octopus is an alien creature, one whose path wandered a long way from our own.

"For thine is the," Claire murmurs, hears Lily's fork drop, leans down to grope for it, chin to the table, swiping once, twice while they work through the power and the glory, picks it up, brushes it against her pants leg and places it quietly next to Lily's plate just in time to say, "Amen."

Gets that puzzled look from Nathan, just a glance—it might have waited, of course, she is distracted. She is always distracted, which is why there is that little bit of hurt behind the look.

"We saw an eel that looked like a pickle yesterday," Lily says. "And a fish that looked exactly like Yoda, didn't it, Mom?"

"A grumpy little Yoda," Claire says.

"That would be disconcerting," Nathan says, smiling.

"They had an octopus," Claire says. "It was so strange."

"It changed colors, just like a chameleon," Lily says.

"I didn't know they changed colors," Nathan says, dishing up some mashed potatoes.

"I know, anyway," Lily says. It's one of the speech patterns she's recently picked up from Samantha.

"By the way, Greg told me today they lost a helper in Kindercare," Nathan says, passing the mammoth potato bowl. "You could work three mornings, or even more if you wanted. He says they could be flexible, too, with the hours. You could just come after Lily makes the bus. We wouldn't have to worry about schedule conflicts." With Claire's museum schedule, Lily has to go to the neighbors' three mornings a week for about ten minutes to wait for the bus.

Claire nods, reaches for the salt. How can she tell him she doesn't want to work with children anymore? That she is tired of toys, of picking them up and cleaning them off, tired of sorting all these odds and ends into endless bins here or at church or—well, yes, at the museum—only to see them scattered across the carpeting again. Although at home it is no longer toys, more books and hair bands and doodads and hoodies and shoes let loose around the house. But she doesn't want to do it anymore, not for a living.

He shrugs as if it doesn't much matter, but adds: "They pay about $10 an hour."

The museum pays her minimum wage. In fact, she started as a volunteer two years ago and has only recently graduated to a paying spot, something they had celebrated with dinner at Friendly's.

"Mom's an astronomer, Dad," Samantha says.

"Well of course," Nathan says, graciously nodding, while Claire runs the math on the pay difference. It's painful: $50 a week, possibly. $200 per month; $2,400 per year. Two-thirds of a trip to Disney.

"I'm not sure I should give up the museum," she says. "They're talking about a new exhibit, and I might be able to help. It could be big." But as the talk turns to school, she is still doing the math. $2,400. Whatever the exhibit will be, she knows, it won't be that kind of big.

Why is it that the chameleon is so famous for its camouflage abilities, while the octopus, the true master of the art of disappearing, is hardly known for it? Unlike a chameleon, which relies on chemicals to change colors, an octopus can change colors and patterns almost instantly using special colored cells called chromatophores that work just like pixels in a TV screen. An octopus can take on an almost unlimited range of pictures and patterns, imitating everything from sand and algae to parrotfish and coral, and can move the patterns at will over its skin. It can show one display on the part of its body facing prey (or a potential mate) while leaving the rest in camouflage. In one common display, the octopus will flash dark stripes over its body in rapid succession; the octopus seems to use it to mesmerize or distract prey. Sometimes, octopuses seem to change patterns merely out of boredom. One study found that the Indo-Pacific day octopus, *Octopus cyanea*, changes body pattern more than two times per minute while foraging.

The octopus's skin can also change texture, from sponge-like and lumpy to smooth. Add to this the octopus's nearly infinite ability to change shape, to flatten and stretch into a sheet or curl up into a ball, and you have a creature that can disappear in almost any environment.

But there's a final element that is essential to the octopus's disappearing act: it is not above acting a part. When threatened, an octopus usually employs a series of coordinated countermoves, some of them reminiscent of old cartoons. The octopus may eject ink, sometimes in the shape of its own body, while it jets to a point nearby and disappears into the scenery. Mimicking a rock, octopuses have been known to creep across the sea floor and freeze every few steps like kids playing red light, green light. When imitating seaweed, an octopus will raise a single, leafy arm into the air and wave it gently in the water like an undulating frond. Some divers have even reported seeing *octopus vulgaris* gather up six of its arms and tiptoe across the sea floor on the other two.

Looking at a picture of an octopus tottering across the sand on its two makeshift legs, the rest of its arms hiked up like frilly skirts, one has to wonder what creature it means to mimic. A can-can dancer? Yosemite Sam? But then the answer is simple—it means only to communicate "biped," as in, "non-cephalopod," which is to say, *anything but me.*

It is fellowship hour at Wheatland, and Claire is at her usual spot by the coffee table, managing with effort an oatmeal cookie and a brimming cup of steaming coffee while keeping tabs on the wayward, aggressive tendencies of her boom swing of a purse. The place is packed. She watches a woman wearing a straw hat with a tidy bow in the back, a docile black snap purse at her side. How does she pull it off? When Claire puts on a hat, she feels like she should be riding on a parade float. The women fascinate her, with their dressy slacks and costume jewelry, their ubiquitous denim jumpers, hair knotted in giant clips. Her aunt had bought her a denim jumper shortly after she moved to Lancaster. It didn't fit: it gripped in some places, gapped in others and was about four inches too long, a familiar problem for Claire because her body is apparently three different sizes at once, so no single item of clothing fits more than about thirty percent of her body at any given time. Except for, well, hats. She'd exchanged the jumper for a sweater, something she could buy without trying on.

A man in front of Claire steps on her shoe. She apologizes and backs up, apologizes again to a woman next to her, who got a poke from her bag, steps back one more time and feels the window sill against her back. She watches the crowd until she locates Lily and Samantha heading back toward the snack table, the highlight of church for them. They'll want a few more minutes, she knows.

She makes her way along the wall to the open door and finds a place to sit on a curb by the parking lot. Outside it's breezy and much cooler than in the fellowship hall. Across the small lawn, the sanctuary stands empty. Tall, clear windows line both walls, so from either side, you can see straight through. The light that comes through the windows is colorless, more like shadow than light. It is the thing she likes best about the place, and the effect is best when it is empty like this, with the light resting on all the wooden pews, the worn wooden floor. Sometimes she even drives over in the middle of the day to look at it.

She fell in love with Nathan here, on the lawn before the church. Fell in love with Nathan and Wheatland and the grand, bending sycamores out front all in one sweet vision, one clear uptake of desire. She saw the beautiful families, the men in their white shirts and ties, the women in their dark sunglasses and bright sundresses, the children, serious, lovely, dressed the same way only smaller, and she wanted to be one of those happy people, walking in the dappled sunlight, strolling contentedly through the grass, looking forward to their picnics or their backyard barbecues, people who knew everyone and were known by everyone. She'd been visiting her aunt, and had come along with her on a whim, and Nathan had come over with a young married couple to introduce himself. She can still see him just as he was then, a lanky, upright figure in a starched white shirt. How earnestly he shook her hand. He had a special khaki holder for his Bible, something she hadn't even known existed before that morning.

This is the place, too, where she thinks she first embarrassed him, or first noticed that she'd embarrassed him, right here in the fellowship hall, picking up Samantha from Sunday school. Samantha had handed her a crayoned picture and Claire asked about the lesson, and when

Samantha told her about it, Claire said, "Zechawho?" Then, laughing, "What's a grown man doing in a tree?" And laughed, and looked up to see that mixed disappointment on Nathan's face, and stopped laughing.

After that she began to notice other things she should be more careful about. Like the one pebble in the movie that sets off the avalanche, that one look on Nathan's face. It had never occurred to her before that morning that a sense of humor could be such a low-down thing. And yet it was, at least her particular brand of it. It wasn't just the joking around, the endless, running sarcasm that constituted her thinking, but the gestures and even the voice that went with it. She was too animated in her speech, and too loud. Then she noticed her diction, too, was sloppy. What she said, plus how she said it. She tried to slow down, to speak deliberately and gently, to modulate her voice. To rein herself in, speak less, think first. Although it was hard, especially in the beginning, after being with the kids all day, when Nathan would finally come home. They talked about that in the moms' groups, how men talked to adults all day, and came home tired of talk, and then the women, who talk more anyway, jump on them at the door looking for adult conversation. They had answers for all those things. They were the most functional people Claire had ever met.

Claire believed in self-improvement. And she improved. There was so much she didn't know, everywhere things she didn't know that everyone else just took for granted. Zechariah. Prayer chains. Theme parties. Bringing dinner to people when they're sick or suffer a setback or have a baby. These were, evidently, the hallmarks of a normal life, and Claire took to them eagerly, gratefully. Having moved a lot as a kid, Claire had a vision of a normal life that drew heavily on the Dick Van Dyke show. Friends came by at least weekly for dinner parties, where they did impromptu skits for one another and sang at the piano and joked about the time when Laura burned the roast. There was a lot of Mayberry USA in there, too. Claire imagined it, and then worked toward getting it as methodically as one learns any kind of skill. It was a campaign. Sewing. Raising backyard vegetables. Doing dishes immediately, drying them and putting them away. Reading the paper on Sunday afternoon, still in your good clothes. She saw herself doing these things, did them, and for more than a decade, she was happy. She worked in the nursery, even taught a few Sunday school lessons when the main teacher was out. When her girls graduated into older classes, she had stayed on with the little kids because they always needed extra hands with them. For a time, she had even held a key to the front door of the place, a perk of volunteering to collate and staple the programs every Saturday night.

Then one morning during questions and answers in her Sunday school class, a six-year-old boy in a vest and tie was talking about Josiah the Boy King, and Claire realized she was intimidated by him. Not just by him, but by them all, the girls in their lace socks and jumpers, their touching prayers, lisped and rasped out during free prayer time, sometimes so quietly you had to lean in to hear them. And not just the children, but the parents, too, all the things they knew, the things they would always know, the things they were able to take for granted. She had learned what to say: in spring, ask about summer plans, in summer, ask how the trips were going, in fall, ask what teachers their children got, and later how they liked them and how they were adjusting. Around holidays, ask about holiday plans. She had never seen her way past any of that chatter into a real conversation with anyone, just as she had never made it beyond the theme party rounds with any of the women there into anything like friendship, let alone weekly singalongs. The people here, she finally concluded, were of a piece, and her personal attempts at reform aside, they were as foreign to her after a decade as they were on that first visit. Lately, she finds herself thinking about the strangers she met at the AA meetings she attended for a while after college, the black days before Nathan. She had shared something with those people, hunched over their Styrofoam cups of coffee, ritualistically working their cigarettes, with their scrappy benedictions, their hopeful recitations, *Take what works, leave the rest, Don't give up, keep coming back!*

Nathan is the one who belongs here. He's the one who can call on some of the guys when he wants to talk over a problem or go biking. And he rarely even makes it to church now because of his work, which involves a lot of travel. Not that he wants to travel. For years he's been trying to move up into a management position, but his boss is always putting him off, saying it's just around the corner.

It was almost a relief when she finally began to give up her church duties one by one. She stopped attending the women's studies and moms' groups and retreated into her own private take on motherhood. It has been a flawed pursuit, she knows. She is inconsistent. She suffers from a constitutional lack of authority and conviction, often spoils the girls. She jokes too much, loses her temper, can be suddenly hostile when pushed. And she sees now that despite her best efforts, she has probably taught her daughters to question too much and laugh too hard and talk too loudly and opine too heartily and take things too hard and invest too much in every single person on the planet and every last wretched passing thing, and basically set them up to be just like her, which means she has failed, failed at the most important thing, failed them utterly.

The extravagant gestures, she gets. She has painted the girls' rooms three times apiece, each paint job an homage to fairies or horses or creatures of the sea. She makes elaborate costumes at Halloween to transform them into whatever has captured their imagination that season, their dream of the moment. Loves their dreams, their fancies almost as much as they do. Has made every Disney princess out of fondant. She is a pancake artist, ladling out bunnies and snowmen, pumpkins and ghosts. Big wobbly stars. That's what she teaches the kids, you're a star, you are good. Then she realizes, that's just what her mother taught her. And she never believed a word of it. And now, well, now she will just pass it on, her *self,* just like a disease.

> To find out if octopus arms have minds of their own, the researchers cut off the nerves in an octopus arm from the other nerves in its body, including the brain. They then tickled and stimulated the skin on the arm. The arm behaved in an identical fashion to what it would in a healthy octopus.
>
> — "Octopus Arms Found to Have 'Minds' of Their Own," John Roach[3]

The octopus learns by touch, more so than any other cephalopod. Information from receptors in the suckers on the arms travel to the highest learning centers in the brain.

On the level of the arm, though, the octopus has trouble distinguishing position. It must rely on its eyes to tell it what the arms are doing, and even so it has trouble processing what the arms are up to, where they are in space from moment to moment. This may be due to the vast, nearly unlimited range of movement of the arms, what robotics scientists call "manipulative redundancies." To manage the processing load required to simultaneously operate eight arms, the octopus has more neurons in its arms than in its brain, and in fact the arms can function without referring to it. Their arms, in other words, think.

Maybe stranger yet, an octopus's arms also taste. Every sucker is equipped with 10,000 chemoreceptors that can taste chemicals at 10 to 1,000 times lower concentrations than humans can.

As for hearing, despite extensive neurological testing, it remains a topic of some debate whether octopuses are deaf. Recent studies suggest that they respond to shocks associated with low-frequency vibrations, or "infrasound," but no consensus exists as to whether this qualifies as hearing. The octopus does not seem to have the human equivalent of ears; instead, it seems to feel sound with the same receptors that control balance and orientation.

Curiously, researchers believe that despite its unparalleled ability to color match its environment, the octopus is most likely color blind. While its camouflage relies heavily on reflective cells that mirror the surrounding environment, the remainder of the work falls to colored cells directly controlled by the optic lobe. Some believe that by merely matching the brightness, which octopuses are very keen at registering, the colors come close enough. Maybe they see black and white so well that it translates to color. It is strange, though, even taking into account 400 million years of evolutionary meandering in the dark, that the octopus would be blind to something so central to its being, and so significant in its environment. And so beautiful.

It has been clearly established in the laboratory, however, that octopuses can feel pain and do learn in response to it.

One of the biggest shocks of Claire's recent years came at a campout last fall with Lily's Girl Scout troop, where she spent the night with nine other mothers and thirty-two girls. The camping "cabin" was a dated, cement block building reminiscent of a third world clinic, utilitarian to the point of being toxic to the human spirit, the upstairs rooms crammed end to end with metal bunk beds. After a sleepless night brought on, Claire believed, by the despair that was issuing forth from the walls like radon, she unbagged her electric coffee pot, carried it in her arms down to the kitchen and brewed some coffee. She gave a cup to another mom and cracked some joke about the place, or about their weekend getaway (because she is incurable, especially under extenuating circumstances), and the other mother shrugged and said, It is what it is. Not wearily, but not contentedly, either. With *resignation*, Claire decided afterward, only more neutral than that. And then another mother had said it to her this spring, while serving snacks to the cast at the talent show, the very same sentence, in the very same way. *It is what it is.* With a slight smile, the same shrug. It was like some kind of universal telegraph. Claire couldn't quite say what it was about the statement that she found so intractable, so shocking, even. It was as if the thought, this very patent thought that had obviously occurred to everybody else, had simply never occurred to her. And maybe it hadn't.

But lately she thinks she is beginning to understand it. Every year over Memorial Day weekend, Nathan's family has a big campout where more than a dozen families bunk up in campers parked out on his uncle's farm. Most of the family is Mennonite, although many have gone Brethren or independent like Nathan's parents. The cousins are good to Samantha and Lily, even though they don't see them as much as many of the other cousins. They show them all over the farm, give them pony rides, catch kittens for the girls to hold. Knowing they are safe and happily occupied outside, Claire settles into a chair by the fire and listens to other people's stories, watches the fire die during the day and grow at night. Here, no one expects much from her. No one much cares what she wears or how she talks or what she says. They find perfectly crazy ways to occupy themselves—blindfolded tractor races, wheelbarrow races, pie eating contests, including one particularly messy variation involving finding a gumball in the filling—and they pursue the games with serious competitive fervor, employing judges and citing prior year decisions with the exactitude of Supreme Court justices. No rules, no game. They seem to get it, how to spend time, how to strip away all the drive from it and just enjoy it for what it is, and this fascinates Claire, because of all people, they are the last to believe that a single thing on the planet "is what it is." But maybe it's precisely because of that, because they always have one foot in the next world, that it's so easy for them to take this one as it comes.

It's infectious, addictive. By Saturday evening, when they take their two-hour hayride through the back roads of eastern Lancaster County, Claire hunches on a bale of straw and just watches. She watches the empty roads go by, the blind white pea of the moon combing tirelessly through the branches overhead, the people reduced to flashes of faces and arms in the dark, their words drowned out by the insistent chug of the tractor. Waves of heat from the engine, followed by waves of cold, wash over them while the wagon jostles and shakes. The deer they occasionally startle in the fields are white as ghosts.

When Monday comes, she doesn't want to leave. It's strange, she knows, but each year she feels more and more like she should stay out there. Driving home, she asks Nathan, just floating the idea, "Do you ever think that maybe we belong in the country?"

"Yeah," Nathan says, laughing.

"No, really," Claire says. "It's peaceful."

"I'll move there," Lily calls out from the back seat.

"No way," Samantha says.

"Could we get a horse then?" Lily asks.

"We're not moving," Nathan says. "We're just talking." He drives for another minute, and Claire thinks he's dropped the subject when he says, "Last year, you wanted to move to the city."

Maybe it's just the way he says it, or maybe the pauses he's leaving in between, what he must be thinking, but she feels baited. It was two years ago, in fact, when she was looking into graduate school. The nearest programs were in Philly and Baltimore.

"Before that it was the rocky coast—remember, after Maine? And then you wanted someplace with sidewalks, so you could walk to a café."

She looks at the fields spinning past, the unsteady rows split into the earth, the leaves just spiking up from the clay. The car slows and they turn down the road toward their development. He looks over and pats her hand. "It takes work to be content, Claire," he says, gently squeezing. "It doesn't come naturally to anyone."

"I'm not saying we should move," she says. "I just wonder sometimes if we'd be happier if we lived—"

"I know," Nathan says, sighing. "Anywhere but here."

The octopus's ability to squeeze through even the smallest opening makes containing an octopus problematic, even for professionals. Tales of their legendary escape abilities are told by research scientists, aquarists, pet owners, and even the occasional fisherman who, having discovered an octopus raiding the day's catch, has tried to add it to the bin. One octopus named Sid went missing from the

Dunedin Aquarium in Sydney, Australia for five days. He hid out in the filtration system until one of the keepers caught him making a run for the door. Some aquarists recommend enrichments such as puzzle boxes to help deter escape, while others believe the added stimulation has the opposite effect. Some recommend a vertical stretch of Astroturf, which the octopus cannot suction onto, at the top of the tank; however, others note that smaller octopuses will use the same material as a ladder to climb out. Whatever the tactics, it is commonly understood that if there is a way out, an octopus will find it and take it.

There's a universal physics of escape, and even the earth is subject to it. To escape gravity, the planet's grasp, an object must be traveling at least 11.2 kilometers per second, or 25,000 miles per hour, the earth's escape velocity. The funny part is that that is also the *enter* velocity: an object can neither come in nor get out unless it is traveling at least that fast.

The greater the mass, the greater the escape velocity. Jupiter, with a mass 316 times that of the earth, has an escape velocity of 60.24 km/sec, or 132,000 miles per hour, so Jupiter has rarely been hit. Whatever comes near, it just shoves out of the way.

The moon's mass is one eightieth of the earth's, and its escape velocity is only about 2.37 km per second, or 5,000 mph, which is why it is what it is. Hammerland.

The same physics applies to people. During the first election of George W. Bush, commentators noted that people were naturally drawn to him because he was "comfortable in his own skin." His running mate, Dick Cheney, was said to have "gravitas."

It was just another thing to feel bad about.

A comparison of the Daily Cycles of *Octopus vulgaris*
and *Sepioteuthis sepioidea*, the Caribbean Reef Squid

Octopus:	Squid:
Day: 12%: morning feeding & foraging	Day: 10%: morning migration
70%: asleep or resting	64%: shoaling
3%: home maintenance	8%: predator avoidance
3%: other unknown activity	8%: courtship & mating
12%: evening feeding & foraging	10%: evening migration
Night: 100%: unknown activity	Night: 100%: feeding & foraging

—*Cephalopod Behaviour*, Roger Hanlon &
John Messenger[4]

So things have begun to slip. After more than a decade of being careful, of clipping coupons and comparison shopping and packing sandwiches and carrot sticks for trips and hanging out the wash, being a good home economist, Claire has begun to forget things. She has stopped counting her change, tries to use coupons but somehow can't keep up with the expiration dates, has given up comparing the circulars that come with the paper to see which store has the best deals each week. She slides her ATM card and walks out of the store with a cart stacked full of the same items week after week. They run out of something almost daily now; no sooner does she remember toilet paper than they run out of shampoo, or scotch tape, or ammonia, or lettuce or milk. What they don't run out of, breaks. The coffee pot. The vacuum. Or things on Nathan's list: faucet gaskets. Toilet flappers. She has stopped making lists, which she always left on the table next to the coupons anyway. She walks the grocery store like an ant on a scent trail, letting the shelves remind her of what she needs, coming back the next day for what she missed. Nathan looks at the house and says, "Cut back your hours if you need to. We don't really need the money."

~ ~ ~

Octopuses are the only cephalopods that build burrows. They spend between five and twenty-five minutes building a den by piling up rocks and blowing out sand with their siphons. They will also adapt existing materials into a home, and are particularly fond of split coconut shells, which they duck into and reassemble, opening and closing the two halves like a front door. (Scientists disagree on the question of whether this repurposing constitutes genuine tool use). They're irresistibly drawn to all the junk we throw overboard, bottles and cans, traps and pots, which makes it unfortunately easy to catch a wild octopus. They have a special affinity for aluminum cans, so much so that sea otters regularly tear cans apart hunting for octopus inside.

What drives them so reliably into artificial shelters can only be guessed at. It could be a purely practical response: a tidy aluminum-sided house is more secure than a cobbled-together rock heap. Or it could go deeper, tapping into some latent, 400 million-year-old memory of the shell they gave up. Or maybe it is simpler than all that: the octopus sees a nice, smooth bottle, a shiny can. Sees an opening, cannot resist feeling in through that hole, feels the smooth, round space inside and has to go in. Inside, it admires the perfect home, the safe, almost impervious little holder, sized just right for itself. Nice.

Then it spies, what?

The keyhole it came in through. A light, a promising space, a world out there. And, love, *out it goes.*

> The octopus is a stupid creature, for it will
> approach a man's hand if it be lowered into the
> water.
>
> —Aristotle[5]

It is puzzling that the octopus is a solitary creature for a couple of reasons. One, biologists have struggled to explain how a solitary creature with such a short life span could have developed the level of intelligence it seems to have when so much learning occurs socially. Two, in captivity, octopuses are incurably social: they are compulsively drawn to people, and to the puzzles, toys, treats and tortures people in laboratories invariably present them with. Because of this, they have become the lab rat of the cephalopod world.

The octopus, for better, for worse, is a game creature. It cannot help itself.

Although it is reliably curious, the octopus is not always consistent in the laboratory, which is why so many questions about their basic abilities remain unanswered despite their extensive use in research. One laboratory reported that an octopus seemed to dislike a certain researcher and squirted him in the face whenever he approached its tank. When the researcher returned to the lab after more than a month of absence, the octopus squirted him again. Yet study results regarding octopus's visual memory and learning abilities are inconclusive and often contradictory. As a result, opinions within the scientific community vary widely on whether octopus is really all that smart after all, even for an invertebrate.

For a week, Lee has been working to create the perfect environment for the gestating turtle, but she has neglected to dig a nest, despite having eight inches of terrarium moss and bark and an assortment of branches and rocks spread in her tank. Overnight, she laid her eggs on top of the moss, not even together.

"They're probably infertile," Lee says. "I'll give them a few days, but I think they're duds." He pulls her watering tub and replaces the lid, and Claire follows him to the back room where they have a laundry sink and basic supplies for taking care of the animals.

"We got the Tremblay grant," Lee says. "Half is going to that new curriculum, but we have a good budget for an exhibit to replace Human Cultures—I know, hallelujah—what the hell?" he says, lifting from the sink a container with something black in it.

"Somebody's lunch?"

He squints at it. "Let's hope not. Anyway, basically we have carte blanche. So think about it, if you would. I asked Jane to get some ideas together before the weekend, but I know what she's going to say, because she's been after that mechanical energy exhibit ever since she saw that Rube-Goldberg lab out in Pittsburgh. Not that it's a bad idea—it's great, but we can do that with the Dream Machine space. It's already halfway there. No matter what we do, I want to have it planned out by next month so we can get started."

He finishes the tub, refills it and heads back to the exhibit room. Claire sees that Gomer is twisted in the middle, draped dramatically over his artificial log, tail high in the branches, head hanging down in the sawdust.

"Light would be really cool," he says, opening the turtle's cage, carefully lowering the tub. "I'd love to have a subtractive color booth. But I think we should try to keep some social or at least human dimension, since it's replacing cultures."

"What about perceptions?" Claire says. "I just read an article about how we process hearing. Someone played a recording of words with the initial sounds removed, and people filled in the missing sounds based on the context of the sentences they were given. In one sentence, the person heard 'goat,' in the next sentence, the person heard 'boat.' But both times, the recording only played 'oat.'"

"So they've actually proven that people hear what they want to hear," Lee says, laughing, wiping his hands on his pants. "Nice. But I could see it—it's sort of like the Simons-Chabris test, where the gorilla walks out on the basketball court and no one sees it because they're too busy looking at the game."

"Right."

"I like it—but how would you make that into exhibits? And how can we tie it together? Think about it," he says. "And send me that article, if you think of it. It sounds fun."

"Are you going to be here Thursday for Samantha's match?" Claire asks, warming up her coffee and coming over to join Nathan at the table.

He looks up from his computer. "I'll be here all week. I may have to go to Altoona Friday, though."

"She was talking about camp again, but I'm not sure I liked that last program. Most of the kids were so much younger. I think she was the only teenager in the entire camp. But the other one is an overnight, and I don't know . . ." She realizes that he's absorbed in the computer again.

He hears the silence, looks up. "So she wants to do camp?"

"Yes, but I'm not sure we should go back to the Rec, and I found one other, but it's an overnight."

He shakes his head. "No overnight."

"I'm not sure what else there is," Claire says. "And I asked Lily about camps, but she's all over the place. There's a dance camp, but it's all day, and after sitting at a desk eight hours a day for the whole year, I'm not sure it's a good thing for a kid in the fourth grade to . . ."

She waits. It's a petty thing, but she's taken to testing him lately, waiting to see how long it will take him to notice when she stops talking.

He taps a few times and looks up. "What about soccer camp?"

"Oh, I already signed her up for that. But that's just three evenings," Claire says. "I thought she could do another one."

"I think she should pick one," Nathan says. "One camp per year."

"But it's so short," Claire says. "It's not even really a camp. It's more of a clinic." Then she realizes, this is just how it happens. He draws a line and she stretches it. "It's funny, they call everything that happens between May and August a camp. It can be a one hour cooking class, but if it happens over the summer and involves kids, it's camp." She folds the dishtowel into a little triangle, unfolds it. "There should be some kind of standard, don't you think? Like, you know, if it has a campfire, it's a camp. Otherwise, it's a class."

Nathan nods, smiles.

"I'll have to talk to them both some more." She smoothes the towel over on itself, absently folding and unfolding it.

He types, hits return. Just then there's a tiny thunk at the picture window. Another backyard bird mistaking it for a passage. She frowns, feeling vaguely guilty.

"We're opening a new exhibit at the museum," she says after a minute.

"On astronomy?"

"No, something to replace that awful Neanderthal exhibit." Nathan smiles, shakes his head. "They're still deciding what to do, and Lee asked for suggestions. We were talking about something on the five senses."

"That could be cool," Nathan says. His eyes fall back to his inbox—his boss called twenty minutes ago with a problem that Nathan is trying to iron out by email.

"Did you find what he needs?" Claire asks.

"I think so," Nathan says. "So, exploring the senses? Is that what you're thinking?"

"More how we process things, how what we think we see or hear is usually a shorthand for something much more complicated—how our brains cut corners for us. There's this one test where they show someone a video of basketball players out on a court, and they ask the person to count the times they pass the ball, and a gorilla comes out . . ."

Yes, the poor man is trying to earn a living and, yes, his job sucks in many ways, and, yes, he does care, but—

One thousand one. One thousand two. One thousand three. One thousand four.

The stove buzzes. Claire picks up her mug and heads back to the kitchen.

"Is it supper?" Nathan asks, typing a few keys, gathering his papers. "Do you need some help?" and he is getting up and calling for the girls as she answers yes, yes, yes.

Habituation, which is often thought of as the simplest kind of learning, is the relatively persistent waning of a response as a result of repeated stimulation without any kind of reinforcement. A particularly clear example is reported by Wells & Wells (1956): a Perspex cylinder placed on the arm of a blind octopus will be passed under the web to the mouth, where it may be examined for as long as 20 minutes before being rejected. If the same object is repeatedly passed to the arm at intervals of two minutes, the octopus stops passing it to the mouth after two to four trials, stops pulling it towards the mouth after another three to five trials and after

> another four to ten trials spends only four seconds
> examining it. Finally, the arm is withdrawn from the
> object after the briefest of examinations.
>
> —*Cephalopod Behaviour*, Roger Hanlon &
> John Messenger[6]

They claim a crowd of 30,000, although it doesn't seem that big. Nathan came by earlier in the day to lay out blankets and chairs, so they have a good spot close to the band shell, where Maestro Bill Sterzniesk, in a jaunty ball cap and tuxedo, is giving his annual speech connecting the "1812 Overture" to the Fourth of July. He's working it, saying something about freedom, about liberation from large encroaching powers of destruction and oppression, about the universal desire to be free, the instinct to love one's country.

He needn't. Everyone here knows that he plays it so Mayor Gingerich can fire off his collection of fourteen genuine Civil War cannons. A crowd is already lined up at the rope stretched before the cannons, all the young people who feel immortal. Claire wonders if they have hearing protection, at least maybe cotton balls stuffed in their ears. She still wonders about bringing the children here, whether they should all be wearing earplugs, but when she said that the first year Nathan just laughed and said, in an uncharacteristically cavalier moment, what would be the point?

The children have reached the age when they bring friends to these events. Sitting behind them, after more than a decade of being divvied up between them, arms filled with little bodies and bags of snacks and wipe containers and juice boxes and toys, she and Nathan are paired off again, chaperones cradling cameras and soda cans. His sister and her family canceled at the last minute, leaving him and

Claire alone. Samantha and her friend are taking pictures with a new camera, while Lily and her friend are rolling around on the blanket bugging them, sending a deck of cards and a package of Twizzlers scattering.

She watches a man about her own age seated in a folding chair two rows before them, looking happily at his feet. From their pallor it is clear he does not often liberate them from their shoes, and he turns them this way and that, evidently delighting in them. Beyond the band shell is the pond that Samantha once drove her bicycle into; to the right is the woman with the trembling, bipolar Chihuahua who is always stationed next to the ice cream line, ensuring that hordes of small, hapless children will try to pet it.

She watches Nathan watch the orchestra. He has a new line forming at the edge of his mouth, a smile line, and his hair is graying at the temple. It suits him. She reaches out and cups the back of his neck, thumbs his hairline. He looks up, startled, and takes her hand in both of his, gives it a squeeze. She squeezes back and they sit for about thirty seconds before a terrible self-consciousness descends. It's just awkward, she thinks, holding hands at this age. What's worse, she quickly realizes, even more awkward, if that's possible: figuring out how and when you're supposed to let go.

Male and female octopuses alike die after mating. Sometimes the female will eat the male, as spiders do. It will be the last thing she does eat, and it's all part of the pact, no offense intended, no hostility involved, not even a matter of appetite. The pact is to reproduce and die; the female just hangs around a little longer, has work to do. She fertilizes the eggs herself, then strings them up like laundry on a line, hangs them in her den. In some species, she takes sperm packets from various males who've offered them over the past few months and squeezes them out over the eggs like toothpaste.

She hovers over the eggs, fanning them to ensure that they have enough oxygen. Once the eggs are fertilized, the female never leaves the den. She no longer feeds, but continuously cleans and aerates the eggs for one to three months, possibly a quarter of her life span. By the time the eggs hatch, she is emaciated; soon after, she dies. Males who aren't eaten die at about the same age, not from disease or even old age, but because that is what their bodies are programmed to do.

After a full morning with two camp groups, Claire finds Lee in the Human Cultures exhibit, examining the fixtures. It's hard to say how it is possible for cavemen to look dated, and yet the ones here manage to do so. Is it the colors? Claire wonders, looking at the faded painting of savannah behind the figures. They do resemble the green-tinted Kodachrome colors from the pictures of her childhood. Or is it the desiccated furs, or the brutish expressions on their faces, the rendering? The vision, the conception itself of what constitutes primitive man?

"Alas, poor Jim," Lee says, standing before the lead Neanderthal. "Such a sharp dresser."

"Do you ever wonder what it really is that makes things look dated?" Claire says. "Like, how can something like a typeface look dated? And yet they do."

"I know," Lee says, studying the picture alongside her. "I've wondered that. Illustrations, especially. I wonder if anyone has tried to quantify it, what aspects are most subject to, to falling out of fashion. Now that would be interesting. So, anyway," Lee says after a moment. "I know you're only here till noon, but I've got a layout sketched out, and I thought we might look at it over lunch. My treat," he says, smiling in his goofy way, eyebrows raised.

"Oh, I can't," Claire says. "The girls are home, and I have to make a stop—"

"That's fine," he says. "Maybe we can talk next week, before opening."

"Sure—thanks, though," Claire says, and leaves him there with Neanderthal Jim and his unfashionable clan. She signs out and heads across the parking lot, fishing for her keys, the whole time wondering, lunch? What does that mean, exactly, to be asked to lunch? She shakes those thoughts away. Lee is happily married—his wife is a professor, a cellist. Probably people in their world go out to lunch all the time—men, women, it probably doesn't matter.

Yet she knows exactly what Nathan would say about it. Nathan would be clear on this. Married men and women do not make friends, he would say. They do not go to lunch.

But if she could—would she go? Does she really want to?

She thinks about it for a moment, knows the truth, and it is disheartening and exhilarating and sad: she would love to go.

> It is easy to identify the home of *H. lunulata* or any Octopodidae: The area immediately in front of the opening is littered with the shells and hollowed-out legs of various crustaceans. It occupies a particular nest for a long time and ventures forth only to hunt for food or look for a mate. However, it cannot resist a new nest when one is offered.
>
> —"Hapalochlaena Lunulata," Kelly Ray[7]

Picture her standing next to Nathan in fellowship hour, talking about summer trips taken or planned, in a dress that is attempting to go Jackie-O and a figure that is decidedly not, her hair kinking up into wayward tendrils in the humidity. She is finding it harder all the time to maintain eye contact, to keep from stammering, to keep from squinting, to find things to say. She looks through the back windows of the hall to the windows of the sanctuary, and to the tiny squares of green that mark the lawn on the far side. Longs to spend this hour in the cool of the sanctuary, in its silence, in that sinking, absent light.

She is not sure that she has pulled it off, the normal life she intended for the girls. She does not belong here, and she is not sure they will ever really belong here, either. And she isn't even sure, anymore, that she wants them to. Among all the possible lives, is this really the best one? Has she given them the best? Or has she just created another minor suburban ruin, a stunted, discontented home which they will, in their own time, flee to make way for a better one, to correct the errors of their own histories?

"Excuse me," she says to Nathan, and he nods, smiling, but watches as she makes her way toward the door. Within minutes, he comes out of the hall after his wife, who is standing in the yard with grass stuck to her heels, holding the building up with her back, holding the world out before her, a bit of sky reflected, trembling, in a Styrofoam cup.

That's all it means, Deuteronomy, the sins of the father. *Errors become code.*

She remembers moments: the bag of bread on the milk box, reaching, being stung. Fearing the milk box. The dress she wore to second grade, standing in another doorway. How they always kept you in the office until some awkward hour, and then marched you down the silent hallways into a closed room, interrupted the entire class to say, always mid-lesson, everybody, look. A new student. Her impossible last name, not even the teachers could pronounce. Shame. All those eyes looking up at once, thinking—what?

That had been the start of it, yes, searching faces for what they wanted, what they expected. She had spent so much time reading people's faces over the years and trying to deliver whatever they were looking for that she sometimes interrupted people to tell them what they wanted to hear. Underneath, she was a blank, a fraud.

"Does it know what it is, do you think?" she asks the Instant Ocean man, her hand rounding the corner of the tank, the octopus, fluid, ghostly, trailing it. What is worse, that it knows, or that it doesn't know?

"You mean is it self-aware?" he says, smirking because he's a bit of a smartass, one of those underemployed know-it-all geeks. "It's pretty hard to say what it knows, wouldn't you say? But we do know this much: it knows *where* it is, and it remembers where it's been. They've done experiments with mazes. Just like rats," he says, taking a screwdriver to his Instant Ocean bin, a big knuckled white bucket that releases with a loud pop.

"I read that they turn white when they're afraid," Claire says. The Instant Ocean man ignores this.

"But it can't be afraid, because why would it come?" she says.

It is clearly relaxed, hanging on the glass, the ends of its arms curled into spirals like little locks of white hair, eyes in slits. The Instant Ocean man told her once that the octopus is always squinting in here, that the lights are too bright. That when you turn out the lights, its eyes round out. She wishes that she could see it that way, eyes wide open in the darkness. What it looks like when it is at home with itself.

His boss calls at 10:30 on a Saturday morning. Claire suspects he has no intention of ever moving Nathan out of his technician spot, because no matter what he says, every time there's a system failure or a tie-up or a glitch, Nathan is the one they call. Nathan is trying casually, genially to avoid another trip without upsetting his boss. He has a big day planned, a bike ride and a picnic down by the river; their lunches are already packed. She hears his voice waver on the phone, feels something like the shift of continental plates in her chest, stands up and sets aside her coffee cup and walks into the kitchen, where he is attached to the wall because no one can ever find a handset in this place, presses her forehead into the back of his shirt, the angles between his shoulder blades, and wraps her arms around his stomach. She stays there, smelling him, feeling his voice through her skull, listening with her bones. He turns, unwinds the springy cord over his head.

He never sees her leave, so he can never see her come back.

An octopus has three hearts, and maybe that explains everything. One is here, the true one; it never leaves. The second one is out there in the crowd, grasping faces, turning them left and right, asking every creature the same two questions, the only questions: *Are you alone? Do you see me?*

And the third? The third is abyssal, alone as a star.

On her last visit, the octopus's tank is marked "HOLD-LAYAWAY" in grease pencil.

She realizes now why it is white. It is just turning the color of the things around it, of water and glass and a gray-painted wall. It isn't afraid. It's just making like nothing. She puts up her hand and is almost disappointed when it lets go of its little PVC tube.

"Why does it always come to me?" she asks the Instant Ocean man, and as the octopus rises, predictably, arms outstretched, he shakes his head, gives her that know-it-all laugh and says, "Why do you always put up your hand?"

ENDNOTES

[1] Interesting that the researchers felt obligated to put 'curiosity' in quotes, but not 'frightened' or 'friendly.'

[2] "The Octopus: A Model for a Comparative Analysis of the Evolution of Learning and Memory Mechanisms," Binyamin Hochner, Tal Shomrat and Graziano Fiorito, Department of Neurobiology, Institute of Life Sciences and the Interdisciplinary Center for Neural Computation, Hebrew University, Jerusalem, *Biological Bulletin Online*, http://www.biolbull.org, June 2006.

[3] "Octopus Arms Found to Have 'Minds' of Their Own," John Roach, National Geographic News, September 7, 2001, reporting on the work of Binyamin Hochner, Institute of Life Sciences, Hebrew University, Jerusalem.

[4] *Cephalopod Behaviour*, Roger T. Hanlon & John B. Messenger, Cambridge University Press, 1996, p. 162.

[5] *History of Animals, Book IX*, Aristotle, Translated by D'Arcy Wentworth Thompson, The Internet Classics Archive courtesy of MIT, classics.mit.edu.

[6] Hanlon & Messenger, 138.

[7] "Hapalochlaena Lunulata," Kelly Ray (author), Southwestern University, for University of Michigan Museum of Zoology Animal Diversity Web. Stephanie Fabritius, Southwestern University, Ed.

A note from the author

With abiding thanks . . .

First to Kevin Morgan Watson, for honoring these stories and making them part of the coolest press on the planet. To Bill Black and Tristan Davies, for generosity and genius. To Karen Russell, for being Karen Russell. To Vince Harriman, Nancy Hoffman, and Bobbi Nicotera, for close reads and brilliant advice. To Anniken and Albert Davenport, who basically launched my freelance career. To Jill Barnes, who once drove all the way to Boston to attend a reading and wound up getting towed home to PA. Man, I'm such a liability.

To Catherine Palermo, Margaret Kreps, and Cheryl Taylor Desmond, who hold my dreams as dear as I do and somehow make it all funny. To my father, Robert Palermo, who taught me wonder, dirt to stars.

To Sarah, for the beautiful cover, and to Emily, for not only reading it all but understanding. To Ken, my co-captain, who makes it all okay.

Finally, a nod to the ghosts that wander these pages: my mother, Marilyn Taylor Palermo, whose friendship I miss more with every year; John and Mary Alma Taylor, who played a respectable Bonnie and Clyde; Frank Palermo, who shared his story with me in spectacular Palermo fashion (pie, coffee and a lot of cutting up); Ruth Gonzalez, who showed me the love of Christ.

Love to every one of you, and to aliens and might-have-beens and every creature on the cusp. I see you. I've seen you.

Elizabeth Gonzalez's short stories have appeared in *Best American Nonrequired Reading, New Stories from the Midwest, SolLit Selects, Greensboro Review, Post Road,* and many other publications. In 2011, she received the Howard Frank Mosher Prize from *Hunger Mountain* for "The Speed of Sound," and in 2012 she received the Tusculum Review Prize for "Shakedown." She works as a freelance writer and editor in Lancaster, Pennsylvania, where she lives with her husband and two daughters. *The Universal Physics of Escape* is her debut story collection.

Cover Artist Sarah Gonzalez is a high school senior who plans to study illustration in college toward a career in the field. She is particularly interested in character design and narrative illustration and is currently working on a graphic novel. She is Elizabeth Gonzalez's daughter and by all accounts an all-around great kid. She publishes her work at savictez.deviantart.com

CPSIA information can be obtained at www.ICGtesting.com
Printed in the USA
BVOW05s0247150915

417668BV00007B/18/P